## "It was you who killed our marriage."

Julian spoke passionately. "You who left."

She had to take refuge from his bitterness and from the turbulence in his eyes. "Forgive me, Julian," Liane said wretchedly. "I'll speak to you another time."

"You'll stay here!" He caught at her roughly.

"I must say, you've turned into a tyrant. I will *not* be manhandled." Yet, even as she spoke, her senses were clamoring.

"I remember when you couldn't live without my touch," he told her mockingly.

"Too many knew your touch!"

He held her even tighter, staring down into her eyes. "Can you tell me when I found the time?"

"I can't!" She shook her head, her old griefs rising. "Please, Julian, if you want me to help you with your son, you have to leave me alone!"

**Margaret Way** takes great pleasure in her work and works hard at her pleasure. She enjoys tearing off to the beach with her family on weekends, loves haunting galleries and auctions and is completely given over to French champagne "for every possible joyous occasion." Her home, perched high on a hill overlooking Brisbane, Australia, is her haven. She started writing when her son was a baby, and now she finds there is no better way to spend her time.

# The Hungry Heart

## Margaret Way

# Harlequin Books

TORONTO • NEW YORK • LONDON
AMSTERDAM • PARIS • SYDNEY • HAMBURG
STOCKHOLM • ATHENS • TOKYO • MILAN

Original hardcover edition published in 1988
by Mills & Boon Limited

ISBN 0-373-02999-3

Harlequin Romance first edition August 1989

# CHAPTER ONE

LIANE was always to remember that moment of icy premonition before she answered the low buzz of the intercom. Panic was involuntary but extreme. Julian and little Jonathon sprang into her mind, their images so disconcertingly vivid that pain slashed deep inside. Momentarily she shut her eyes as body and mind dealt with auras she had tried desperately to deny: Julian, the man who had nearly destroyed her; Jonathon, the innocent little boy whose laughter still echoed in her head. Memory was so powerful that the safe citadel she had built herself suddenly collapsed like a sandcastle matched against the swirling tide.

She was back at Sandpiper. Cape Elizabeth in the summer. Jonathon's tinkling laughter, the health and happiness in his adorable sun-kissed face... Julian, that dark and dominant figure filling her life with the sweetest, wildest excitement mortal woman could ever know. Sandpiper. The matchless days of her marriage. Paradise. No more.

The hand that held the receiver wasn't steady.

'Liane, would you come into my office, please?' Her boss, property and investment knight, Sir Eric Mossleigh, spoke tersely into her ear.

Again the rush of panic. The tone was a far cry from Sir Eric's habitual smooth urbanity. Liane stood up like an automaton, smoothing the crease from her pencil-slim skirt. Why did she feel like this, *why*? She had been managing just fine, or as fine as any woman could when her marriage was over. Her breathing had altered and her eyes had gone very large, the pupils dilated. It was *fear* that she felt. She stooped and picked up her notebook and pencil, though she had the certain chilling notion they would not be needed. Something was wrong. She sensed it just as she had sensed tragedy long ago.

Sir Eric, a tall, dynamic-looking man in his early fifties, stood up as she entered, indicating one of the burgundy-leather armchairs with a turn of his hand. His was a palatial office befitting his standing as arguably the country's most powerful tycoon. Ceiling-high windows framed magnificent views of the city, and the panelled walls and the superb antique furniture had once graced an English stately home. The whole effect was that of a distinguished private library, a calculated effect to reduce business friction and put all who entered off guard.

For once Liane did not admire Sir Eric's impeccable taste nor his adroit psychology. She was physically and mentally bracing herself. For *what*?

Sir Eric was looking down at his manicured hands, forceful dark brows brought together in a frown. He was balking at what he had to do just as he knew he had no option. He had never wanted Liane Chantrill for a secretary in the first place. From the moment he had laid eyes on her he had wanted her for his wife. At the age of fifty a miracle had come into his life. He had fallen in love for the very first time. No one suitable, but the last woman in the world he should desire. He had fallen in love with the bride of his bitterest enemy, though both of them kept that profound enmity rigidly under wraps. To most of the world they were corporate warlords, keen rivals in high-powered business deals that ranged internationally. Few people outside Eric Mossleigh had a glimpse into what drove Julian Wilde. Not success, power and all that money could buy, but *revenge*. That was their secret. Now the woman between them looked up at Sir Eric with sea-coloured eyes that had darkened to jade in sharp anxiety.

'Something is wrong, isn't it?' she asked in her low, thrilling voice. 'Please tell me.'

He couldn't help himself. He drew a chair close to her and clasped her locked hands with his own. He saw to his horror that her beautiful complexion had turned as white as alabaster, and he swore that one day very soon he would assume control of her life.

'Not as long as *I* live!' A voice in his head spoke so loudly he actually turned his head over his shoulder, fully expecting to see a tall, menacing figure. Didn't he and Wilde have their secrets! Now Sir Eric tried to dispel his deep-seated qualms about Julian Wilde. Seeing Liane like this made him almost insane with impotent rage, but never for one moment did he intend to display it. 'Try to take this calmly, my dear,' he warned her. 'Gower has just alerted me to a newsflash. Much as I loathe upsetting you, I felt you would want to know.'

'It's Julian, isn't it,' she replied, her lovely face filled with abject pain.

Sir Eric flushed, but kept holding her hands. 'I might have known you'd think first of that man. It's not Wilde, my dear. It's his boy.'

'Jonathon?' Liane's silver-gilt head shot up.

Sir Eric's sharp blue eyes narrowed over her as he tried to come to terms with her powerful reaction. 'The newsflash is yet to be confirmed. I've told Gower to get on to the Police Commissioner himself. What we've heard so far is this: someone changed places with Wilde's chauffeur. The boy was picked up from his school at the usual time but not returned to his home. The housekeeper raised an immediate alarm. You know what Wilde's like,' he exploded condemningly. 'He keeps such a high profile that a kidnap attempt wasn't all that unlikely.'

Even in her anguish Liane was startled by his venom. *'No!'* She shook her head violently. 'No one takes better care of his son than Julian.'

'You're more convinced than I am,' Sir Eric returned bluntly, aglow with jealousy. 'Your loyalty, my dear, is inexplicable to me. Look at what the man did to you. *Betrayed* you, when to the rest of us you're as luminous as an angel.'

'I am not speaking for *me*,' Liane answered, barely hearing him. 'Julian would never allow harm to come to his son. Jonathon is everything in the world to him.'

'If you insist.' Sir Eric looked down at her bent head. Always for the office she kept her beautiful blonde hair brushed straight back from her face and neatly clasped at her nape, but once or twice he had seen it tumbling about her face. Once or twice. He wanted desperately to remove the gold clasp, but he didn't.

'It doesn't help when Wilde leads such an opulent life,' he pointed out with a false flash of sympathy. 'The villains in our society feel like taking a slice of the wealth. Wilde has made more money more quickly than anyone else I can think of. He started out at seventeen with nothing but the debts his bankrupt father left him, now at thirty-six he has built a fortune of colossal proportions for one so young. He lives too high and fast, as you more than anyone should know.'

The intensity of her anguish was making his words hazy. 'This is shocking,' Liane whispered, white to the lips. 'My poor, poor little boy.'

'*Another* woman's child, my dear,' Sir Eric pointed out with his customary insistence at getting the facts right.

'I loved him, *love* him, as if he were my own.'

'This has been a terrible shock for you.' Sir Eric allowed himself a warm, comforting caress of her delicately curving shoulder, under its sheath of pure silk. 'For us all. I'm not an admirer of Wilde's, but I do see how a thing like this could destroy him.'

'Does he know?' Liane appeared oblivious of the caressing hand, staring with intensity into Sir Eric's eyes.

'I would say so. He flew back from Tokyo last night. A friend of mine passed that on. His dealings were supposed to take the best part of ten days, but he has prodigious talents for getting what he wants in a hurry. Not that I approve of his methods and the way he curries favour with all-powerful people. No doubt whoever took the boy thought his father would still be out of the country.'

'I wouldn't like to be that person,' Liane shivered.

'Nor I!' Sir Eric seconded in an involuntary admission, at the same time dropping his hand. 'Wilde is the most dangerous man I have ever known. He always had a potential for ruthlessness, even as a boy. He won't leave this to the proper authorities, mark my words. He'll go after the boy himself.'

'Wouldn't you?' Something flared in Liane's huge, iridescent eyes.

'I might *like* to, my dear,' Sir Eric said grimly, 'but I know I would have the discipline not to interfere. The police are the proper people to deal with these situations.'

'Pray God they're working on it now.'

Sir Eric checked himself from touching her cheek. 'You're tearing yourself to pieces, my dear.'

'I'm doing my best to remain calm.' Liane bit on her lip but tears filled her eyes. 'What am I to do? I can't bear to think of Jonathon held against his will. He's such an intelligent little boy. So brave he'll throw out a challenge. It would be better for him if he weren't so bright, so much like his father. He'll notice *everything*. I know he will. It could make for danger.'

'Liane, *please*.' Her distress was tearing Sir Eric's heart out. With the greatest tenderness he drew her to her feet, keeping his arms around her in fatherly fashion. 'Allow me to take you home. Miss Newell can cancel my appointments for the rest of the day.'

'Thank you.' Liane was feeling very faint, but she tried to shake the feeling off. 'Can someone take a child in broad daylight?'

'They can and they do.'

A call came through on the intercom and Sir Eric turned back swiftly to answer it, his handsome face grim. He listened very carefully and uttered one sentence.

'That's what I thought.'

Liane's legs threatened to go from under her and she sat down very quickly, her gaze fixed on Sir Eric's face.

'The news is confirmed, I'm afraid. The ransom demand has already been received.'

Liane was still looking towards him but her vision suddenly blurred. Fear was pumping through her. A crisis of sheer panic. *Jonathon!* Whatever she had expected, she had never expected this. She pictured him bound, frightened. Julian risking everything to get his son back, a Julian so implacable in his purpose he made other men of resolution pale in comparison. She thought her heart would break.

Sir Eric called to her just as she started her slide into unconsciousness. At that point his feelings for her were blazoned all over his face, but Liane never saw them. In a single movement that was incongruously balletic she slipped out of the armchair and came to rest almost gently on the richly glowing Persian rug. Sir Eric rushed to kneel beside her slumped figure, turning her gently and slapping in agitation at her blue-veined wrists.

'Liane,' he murmured, in a low, restrained voice. 'Let me help you.' He exhaled in relief as she opened her beautiful eyes. 'I must get you home. You shouldn't be alone.'

\*     \*     \*

Sir Eric's chauffeur-driven ocean-blue Silver Spur moved regally through the city and out to the leafy garden suburb where Liane lived in the much admired old colonial house her great-grandfather had built. There was little talking in the car. Liane sat with her head tilted back against the plush Connolly leather upholstery, trying to pray, but so sickened that the well-remembered phrases of her childhood wouldn't come together. Finally all she could hold in her mind was a profoundly fervent *Please. Please God, please.*

'Liane?' Sir Eric spoke sharply. 'You're all right, aren't you?'

She turned her head and opened her eyes. 'I'm trying to make contact with God.'

Sir Eric stared at her a little awkwardly. 'The police know what they're doing,' he murmured soothingly.

'And I respect them for it, but I'm putting my faith in God.'

'Perhaps you're right.'

The Rolls glided to a stop outside an enchanting old house which had once been a showpiece but was now in need of fairly extensive refurbishing both inside and out. The original four acres of land had been reduced to just under one acre, allowing room for the modern architect-designed homes on each side. But it was an exclusive area, and the old house would be a joy for someone to renovate. Sir Eric had other plans for Liane.

Richmond, the chauffeur, was lightning-quick in his attentions, opening the door and helping Liane to alight. He had driven Sir Eric's private secretary on many occasions and he had never failed to marvel how anyone as brilliant as Julian Wilde had ever bothered to look at another woman with a wife like that. She was breathtaking in the way he admired most. Very classy and refined. He had seen some sumptuous women in his travels but he still considered Liane Wilde, or Liane Chantrill as she now called herself, the loveliest woman he had ever seen. So serene and graceful. Watching her was like watching a swan gliding across the crystal waters of a lake. She never attempted to make an impression, her beauty was inherent. Simply there. Now pain and desperation were naked in her grave and lovely face. Richmond too had heard the news and been transfixed by it. Powerful people had powerful problems. Sometimes he thought it was downright dangerous to have too much money.

'I'll come in with you for a few moments, Liane,' Sir Eric said solicitously, taking Liane by the elbow.

'Please, you've been kindness itself. I know the appointments you had lined up.'

Sir Eric inclined his handsome narrow head. He would have given anything to be able to take her into his own protective custody. Damn it, he *idolised* her, which increased his perturbation at what was happening to her now. Would she ever get Wilde out of her heart and mind?

'Fifteen minutes, Richmond,' he clipped off.

'Yes, sir.' Richmond, an intelligent and observant man, kept his eyes respectfully lowered. A blind man could see the boss worshipped the ground Liane Chantrill walked upon. Sometimes it seemed to Richmond she had offered him a new life. Richmond admired his boss tremendously but he had never liked him. He *did* like the last man he had been told to trust: Julian Wilde, the only serious pretender to Mossleigh's throne. Wilde was one of the glamour characters of the world. He was never out of the newspapers: the financial pages and the gossip columns. Richmond felt very badly about his little son. So did his ex-wife. Some men, Richmond decided, you just never forgot.

Inside the cool, silent house Sir Eric insisted on making Liane a cup of tea. 'I'll have one with you,' he told her, moving with smooth efficiency around the spacious yellow and white kitchen. 'I know how you like it. Black with a slice of lemon. My wife used to say no kitchen is complete without a bowl of lemons.'

'Do you think there would be any news?' Liane stood in the doorway watching him.

'You must let yourself relax, my dear. I know it's not easy, but making yourself ill is not helping anyone. I have people on it. When there *is* any news I swear to you I'll be here to break it. Now sit down at the table, *please*. This is a very pleasant old house, but much too big for you. You've never considered an apartment?'

'Never.' Sadly Liane shook her head. 'This is my home. My family home. All I have left, really. Besides, Gran is still here. In the house and especially in the garden. She looked after me so wonderfully in life, I know God allows her to stay around.'

'You're too much on your own.' Sir Eric looked back at her sharply. 'Do you never think of remarrying? You're a very beautiful young woman. You're missing out on a normal life. You want a husband, a man who longs to devote his life to you.'

'One marriage was enough.'

'Nonsense, Liane!' Sir Eric looked at her almost sternly. 'You can't allow one bad experience to ruin your life. You were born to be cherished.'

'I was born to trouble,' Liane said wryly. 'Not all that many people lose both parents and at once. I was ten. Old enough to really suffer. Whatever in the world would I have done without truly beautiful grandparents? Then we lost Poppa. Gran and I had to be strong.'

'I quite understand how you came to marry Wilde.' Sir Eric rubbed on his dark moustache.

'The strange thing was Gran really loved him. She told me at the end she had no qualms about leaving me. I had Julian to look after me. She saw him as the perfect choice.'

'He charmed her as he charmed everyone else,' Sir Eric said harshly. 'Not that the charm is too much in evidence these days. He's an exceptionally hard man. I always said he had bad blood. From the father, of course. You did know at one time Jonathon Wilde and I were partners?'

Liane sat down at the kitchen table trying to concentrate on what Sir Eric was saying. 'Yes,' she murmured, toying with her teacup. 'Julian did tell me.'

'Poor devil killed himself, you know.'

'Julian saw it differently.'

'Differently, how?' Sir Eric sat down at the table facing her.

'I don't know exactly. Julian never would talk about his father. Only an odd remark now and again. I knew better than to probe; the wounds were too raw. Julian loved his father deeply, that much I do know. He named his son after him.' She touched her slender white fingers to her aching head. 'Why does tragedy follow some people?'

'Perhaps they provoke it,' Sir Eric suggested raspingly.

Liane laughed abruptly, a hollow little sound without humour. 'God, it's been two years, yet it seems like only yesterday.'

'What does?' For the first time Sir Eric saw passion in the haunted angel face, a passion he alone wanted to arouse.

'I've tried so hard never to let thoughts of Julian enter my mind. Yet today, even *now* I feel he is trying to reach me. I feel *Jonathon* is crying out to me. We were so happy, do you know? A real family: Jonathon loved me. I was the only mother he ever really had. His own mother risked her life to have him and she was never to look on his adorable little face.'

'It never occured to you Wilde should never have allowed his first wife to have a child?' Sir Eric said with intense disgust.

'He didn't know it would be dangerous for her.'

'You accept that?'

'She never told him. Her own sister agrees on that. No one ever blamed Julian. Only himself. Caroline was determined to give him a son and she did. Caroline's family will be distraught with grief now. I should go to Barbra. We have always kept in touch.'

'Yet you never kept in touch with the boy?'

'You must understand. I was no one any more. Julian didn't want me. I had lost his love. Jonathon wasn't my son. I couldn't subject him to all the distress of stepping in and out of his life. I've always sent presents. Christmas, Easter, his birthday. I couldn't not do that. Barbra was always my friend. She was there to console him.'

'From what I hear, the person she really wanted to console was Wilde.'

'Why, who told you that?' Inside Liane trembled violently.

'My dear girl, no one could accuse you of being dumb. It's generally known Barbra Edwards was in the running long before her sister. But then you mightn't have known. You were a lot younger.'

'But Barbra never told me. I don't think you can be right.'

'Well, I don't intend to press it, but gossip had it both Edwards sisters were madly in love with Wilde. Despite her very attractive appearance Barbra Edwards still isn't married and she's well into her thirties. Doesn't that mean something to you?'

'The only thing that means anything to me is that little Jonathon is missing.' A strained silence fell between them.

Later, at the door, Sir Eric had to check himself not to kiss her. Instead he pressed her shoulder. 'I'd like to come back this evening, if I may.'

Liane dropped her eyes. Lately it seemed to her Sir Eric had come to care for her, and she couldn't ignore it. He was a proud and powerful man. There were decisions to be taken. She nodded. What else could she do? He might have news. When Jonathon was safe she would have to rearrange her life. Nine out of ten women of her acquaintance would have been dizzy with triumph if Sir Eric Mossleigh had showed an interest in them but Liane didn't count great wealth a virtue. It was love her heart was hungry for. Love alone had grandeur. She wished for love more than anything else in life. Once she had had it. Surely Julian had loved her? Their brief courtship had been like some splendid fairy-tale. He was already an extraordinary man. She had been so very young, just out of university and working for a public relations firm...

'Wilde is giving a big party for all us good dedicated workers,' Faye Galloway, top woman executive and her immediate boss told her.

'Great!' Liane looked up from an agenda to smile. 'He sure likes throwing his money around.'

'What the hell's money?' Faye joked. 'The faster he spends it the faster he makes it. You're invited, kiddo.'

'*Me?*' Liane stared up at her, startled. 'Since when did junior employees attend big parties?'

'That's what I said.' Faye slipped off the desk. 'Don't look so big-eyed. I think he made up his mind the instant he saw you.'

'What, when I brought in a file? This isn't real!'

'It's real enough,' Faye said ironically. 'What do the romantics call it? A *coup de foudre*. A stroke of lightning, love at first sight.'

'But we never spoke a word,' Liane protested, still floating around his extraordinary ambience.

'Now *that* is what I'm talking about.' Faye wagged a finger.

Her grandmother had been perturbed. They were sitting on the veranda after a light supper enjoying the fragrance from the garden. 'I don't think I like the sound of this, darling. Julian Wilde has asked you to a party?'

'Not me, silly.' Liane leaned over and grasped her grandmother's petal-soft hand. 'Half the office.'

'Did he invite Rosemary?' Celia Chantrill asked shrewdly.

Liane hesitated. 'Not really.'

'Rosemary not pretty enough?'

'Rosemary wasn't really part of the team.'

'From what I hear that man is dangerous.'

'Dangerous?' Even thinking of him made Liane feel hot and excited. 'In what way?'

'Well, he's too attractive for one thing, and too many things seem to happen around him. He lost his poor father in tragic circumstances, then his young wife. It hasn't stopped him from making many friends. He's always in the papers and *always* with some stunning-looking woman. And all this money. How does he make it?'

'The general opinion is he's a financial genius.'

'Are you sure?'

'What are you implying, Gran?' Liane laughed.

'I know for certain he started out with nothing. Jonathon Wilde apparently gambled very rashly on the stock exchange and lost the family fortune; now his son is throwing money around like water. Can one amass all that money in a very short time without becoming involved...'

'In crooked deals? Organised crime?'

'I didn't mean that, Liane. Perhaps a few shady people.'

'Not at all. Entrepreneurs are thrashing the old rich, Gran. It's a wealth bonanza for brilliant young men like Julian Wilde. They're pushing all the illustrious oldies off into retirement. It's the entrepreneurs who are spearheading the accumulation of wealth in this country, and the speed with which they are adding to their assets is phenomenal. Once they were thought rather brash, now they're well on to being billionaires and enormously respected. There are plenty of others. Julian Wilde is emerging as a new leader. You know yourself that the old families who used to dominate the boardrooms are getting out. A new establishment is in the making. For men like Julian Wilde, no corporate pinnacle is too high.'

'And no beautiful young woman is safe. You're not even twenty-two.'

'A few months...'

'And he *has* to be in the early thirties. Why when he married that little girl Edwards, it was the wedding of the year. Such a pretty little thing. What really happened there? There are such a lot of strange stories about that particular man. Oh, I know he's fascinating. I've seen him on the television, handsome as the devil with that striking combination of very dark hair and light eyes, but his life-style is worlds away from ours.'

'I'm only going to a party.'

'Why do you think, darling? You've only been working for Olsen-O'Connell for a very short time. I know Miss Galloway sings your praises, but I feel sure you've been invited for your looks.'

In the end her grandmother gave way and Liane went to the party wearing an enchantingly pretty white taffeta evening dress that was all the gilding her youthful beauty needed. Her long, thick, straight hair made a shining aureole around her face and the emotions that throbbed in her brought a lovely wild-rose colour to her white velvet skin.

The party was in full swing when she arrived. At that time Julian Wilde lived in a magnificent waterfront estate with breathtaking views of cobalt bays and the glorious Pacific beyond. This jewel-like setting was very quiet and private, but tonight, as Liane drove through the manned gates and up the long tree-lined drive, a succession of cars with legendary badges were parked bumper to bumper. This was obviously another one of his parties on the grand scale. Her little red Mazda fitted beautifully into an angle where the Mercedes and Jaguars and a brilliant-looking Rolls couldn't go, and she gave a little crow of triumph. All that stuff about Rolls Royces! Her little darling was a dream to park.

Out on the gravelled driveway she stood looking up at Wilde's spectacular modern mansion. It looked more like a palace within its landscaped five acres bearing stunning witness to his meteoric rise. Lord only knew how far he would go in the future, yet more than one astute observer had gone on record as saying money didn't drive him. The key word, it was suggested, was challenge. His financial genius was already public knowledge.

She was greeted inside the door by Max Olsen Jnr., an unwanted would-be suitor who seized her by the arm. 'Ah, Liane, how exquisite you look!' His snapping black eyes ran over her. 'I was wondering what that mane would look like out; now I know.'

Liane smiled at him but without encouragement. 'I have to say I don't really know what I'm doing here, Max.'

'You're joking!' Max gave her a droll look. 'What good is a party without beautiful girls?'

'Absolutely! Are those beautiful girls allowed to have a brain?'

'Why certainly, darling. But only within office hours.'

Max laughed at his own little joke, a habit, and drew her across the marble-floored, orchid-decked entrance gallery and into the great living-room beyond. Inside the ceilings were so high, the spaces so huge and flowing Liane had to take a moment to adjust herself to the sheer scale. She had been accustomed all her life to living in what was regarded as a large home, but this took her breath away. Furnishings, paintings, Coromandel screens that soared, marvellous lamps and even magnificent indoor plants matched the heroic scale, but then she saw Julian Wilde.

He was standing commandingly, as was his custom—people said he always thought on his feet and his brain never stopped—his back to a spectacular stone fireplace with oriental porcelains lining the mantel. An older man flanked him, silver-haired, ten or twelve people were arranged around him, but Wilde was the natural focus for all eyes.

Liane's first thought was he was too damned much. He really ought to be ugly, with so much else going for him. Instead he was very tall, very lean, with the classic build of an athlete. He looked *quality*, yet his physical impressiveness was quite secondary to his extraordinary charisma. It was almost as if he were enclosed head to toe in an aura not unlike the pictured halo of saints. Except this man was no saint. He was rich, brilliant and darkly handsome until he turned that striking profile and one saw his eyes. They were a complete shock. With his dark hair and deeply tanned olive skin—he was an acclaimed yachtsman—one naturally expected eyes that were either hazel or brown. Instead the remarkable contrast: dazzling blue eyes beneath hair like a crow's wing, the turquoise dramatised by the black. Even the austerity of his meticulously cut features was softened by a mouth with curves that were decidedly passionate. He was at once a contradiction, and totally unlike anyone else Liane had come up against in her life.

Though he had been speaking in animated fashion, one hand slicing the air as he made some telling point, as Max and Liane approached he abruptly broke off.

'Don't stop, Julian,' Max called, but he only stood, arrested, looking at Liane. It was as simple as that. Liane wasn't embarrassed, self-conscious. She looked back into his eyes. After that he carried everything before him. Her grandmother was won over at their first meeting, her own faint little protests that everything was moving so shatteringly fast swept aside. Six months later they were married. As passionate and demanding as he was, he had waited until their wedding night before he took her for the first time. It was glorious, another landscape, but now the dream had turned to nightmare. The man she had once known, her most intimate friend and lover, the man who had gone after her and taken her over as relentlessly as he took over companies, had tired of her even as he made passionate love to her in the night. All that time, during the two ecstatic years of her marriage, she had forgotten that one thing: *challenge*. His need to conquer. Her failure had brought acute suffering into her life.

So Liane sat, waiting for the phone to ring, her skin marble-cold with shock and anxiety. Finally she could stand it no more. She had to see Julian, learn what was happening. How could she just sit there when the little boy she had mothered, who had turned to her for everything, was caught in a frightening trap? Maybe there was something she could do. However bitterly she and Julian had parted, and his anger had been frightful, they had never quarrelled over the child. Julian had even insisted she stay with him for Jonathon's sake. If she couldn't in her 'crass stupidity and utter naïveté' trust him in the face of 'some enemy's ugly games' she should at least learn what commitment was. Jonathon needed her even if he didn't. He had lost all patience with her. He had become violent and hostile. He deplored her lack of trust.

How did one trust a husband who took another woman to bed? Usually the other woman, threatened with an ugly scandal, chose to deny it. Lesley Bannigan had not. Not that the Bannigans had prospered. A few clever moves on Julian's part was all that had been needed to seize control of Bannigan Holdings. Lesley Bannigan was no longer even married to her husband. Tony Bannigan had remarried and she had shifted away. Never mind, there had been plenty of other women to lighten the hectic pattern of Julian's days. His was a powerful sexuality. She and Barbra had almost been like sisters during the brief years of her marriage and Barbra had continued to keep in touch, lending a sympathetic ear. After all, she was Jonathon's aunt, almost another version of his own mother, yet Jonathon, the precocious toddler, had had trouble recognising the close family bond. Many was the time he had actually pushed Barbra away, but then, as Barbra said, Liane was spoiling him with her over-gentle ways.

She rang through to Sir Eric's office, was told by one of her colleagues he was with an important client, so left the message of her change of plans. Her office friend spoke to her in hushed tones. Everyone had heard the news and their thoughts were with her. It was a terrible thing.

In her bedroom Liane slipped on the yellow linen jacket that went over her cream silk blouse and matched her slim skirt. She removed the swag of gold chains that hung around her neck and replaced them with a long single strand of twelve-millimetre pearls. Julian had threatened to strangle her with them if she dared to return them. They had been his wedding present, along with diamond and pearl earrings fit for a princess. They fell almost to her waist, glowing radiantly against skin and silk. Sometimes she hated them. Now they acted as a talisman, something to protect her against his wrath. Why should a man hate her because she couldn't live with his infidelity? Surely such an attitude was irrational? It had left her feeling hopeless and devoid of truth. He had never truly loved her at all, yet all that while their relationship had been extremely passionate. In the end, she had concluded wretchedly that his energies were such that no one woman could satisfy him. To him casual infidelities were simply not an issue. To Liane it was her whole life. Marriage was total commitment; never promiscuous behaviour. The only problem was that in attempting to exorcise him she had locked herself into an ivory tower, a safe place where everything had a false calm. Until now. Under pressure all her deepest feelings surged to the surface, intense, painful, and now that she faced it, unresolved. Julian had assumed a power over her that would never go away.

To her surprise—somehow she had been expecting police cars, the unrelenting media—only a single Wilde employee stepped out of the guard house to the right of the electronically controlled gates. Liane did not recognise him but he apparently recognised her.

'Mrs Wilde?' he queried as he bent to look in at her.

She nodded. A lot of people continued to call her Mrs Wilde. 'Is it possible to go up to the house?'

'I should say so, madam. A shocking business,' he added, his voice lowered but a mixture of rage and helplessness in his face.

'Shocking.' Liane bit her lip but tears filled her eyes. 'Is Mr Wilde there?'

'Yes, madam. My orders are to keep everyone out, but that would not include you.'

I wonder, Liane thought unhappily, watching the man walk back to his box to operate the opening of the massive black wrought-iron gates.

As she drove past she gave him a little wave. There was a desolation in his face anyone would understand, yet had she been a fool in coming here? Would her presence only add to the trauma? According to Barbra, Julian was still saying many bitter things about her, and there was no one quite like Julian to project hostility and anger.

Cars in the drive made up a semicircle. Two police cars were there, four private cars. Liane found that her stomach was quaking, yet she got out of her discreet silver-grey Volvo and walked up one side of the impressive double-entry stone stairway. She had never been in this house. Julian had bought it after he sold Sandpiper. It was a landmark residence in the Mediterranean idiom and the newspapers had reported that Julian had completely re-modelled it as soon as he had moved in. It was even more opulent than Sandpiper, an imposing reminder of a bygone era.

The entry was dramatic, triple arches enclosed by glass leading to the reception rooms of the main floor. A uniformed police officer stood on duty, but unlike the sentry on the gate he instantly demanded her name.

'Liane Chantrill. I was once married to Mr Wilde.'

'Have you identification, Miss?' He subjected her to a searching look.

'Why, certainly.' Liane unclasped her handbag but as she did so, a tall, very slim woman wearing a Chanel suit in a bright shade of strawberry rushed into the plant-filled reception area, her handsome, haughty face a study in shock and incredulity.

*'Liane!'*

'I had to come, Barbra,' Liane explained swiftly, her heart in her eyes.

'You know this lady, Miss Edwards?' the police officer asked.

'Yes, of course.' Barbra frowned at him imperiously, at the same time moving towards Liane and embracing her. 'This is Mr Wilde's ex-wife.'

'Is there any news?' Liane searched Barbra's dark eyes.

'Nothing.' Barbra turned away, obviously in a distraught mood. 'Do you think it was wise to come, Liane? No one could possibly doubt the purity of your motives, but Julian doesn't look on you as part of the family now.'

'Then he's wrong.' Liane's heart pounded loudly but she kept her voice under control. 'I had Jonathon for two years. I was a mother to him. I love him.'

'Please try to keep your voice down, dear.'

'I wasn't aware I was shouting, Barbra.' Liane stared at her. 'Are you unhappy I'm here?'

Barbra took her hand and drew her further down the arched area. 'Liane, dear, you must realise it has nothing to do with me. I have always been your friend. It's Julian we're talking about. He's half out of his mind. The sight of you might put him over the edge.'

Liane drew away. 'I have to go to him all the same.'

'I don't understand you, Liane,' Barbra protested, catching Liane's arm. 'You always dreaded coming into contact with Julian. All he can offer you is more grief.'

'Jonathon is the important one,' Liane said very quietly. 'If there is any way I can help, anything I can do, I must do it. I can't sit at home wondering what is happening.'

'My dear, believe me, you should have remained there. You know you could count on me to contact you as soon as we had news. Here, not only will you be in the way but you risk humiliation. Julian hates you so much he could have you thrown out. How you got past Webber on the gate, I'll never know.'

'He recognised me,' Liane said falteringly. 'Please don't blame him.'

'He was told to keep everyone out.'

'How is it, then, that you got in?'

Barbra started back as if at a blow. 'My dear, you're so upset you don't know what you're saying. Jonathon has no one else. I *am* Jonathon's aunt.'

'Forgive me, Barbra.' Liane leaned her forehead against her fingers. 'You have to think how I feel. Julian and I may have parted, but Jonathon is still part of my life. I send him presents. He is always in my thoughts and prayers.'

'I know, my dear. I know.' Impulsively Barbra bent forward and kissed Liane's cheek. 'You did have a great depth of feeling for the boy, but you must understand Julian would not want you here. There's no limit to his fury at the way you publicly humiliated him. He didn't want the divorce, you will remember. He's a very proud man.'

'If he admires pride, he should appreciate the reasons behind my actions. But why are we talking about any of this now? It's Jonathon who is in danger.' Liane swung away impulsively and Barbra cried after her,

'Come back, Liane.'

Liane ignored her. Despite her trepidation, she rushed across an immense drawing-room like the inside of a jewel-box to a room beyond, from which issued voices.

Five men were in the room, a book-lined, richly toned library taking its colouring from the magnificent garnet-red damask curtains, but Liane's eyes flew to the dominant figure so shockingly, *coldly*, surveying her.

Another man, the senior police officer, spoke to him and Julian answered in a low voice. He moved away from the central book-covered table and walked towards Liane, who was now feverishly clinging to the high back of an antique chair to support her.

'Julian.' She held out her hand not so much in greeting as to ward him off.

'No one behaves more oddly than you do. What are you doing here?' he demanded.

'I had to come.' There was a catch in her voice. 'Jonathon is important to me.'

'Really?' Under the coldness was a latent ferocity.

'I told her not to come in here, Julian.' Barbra rushed in to them, her voice defensive.

'Please, Julian,' Liane said. She felt so faint she could barely stand up.

'You need a drink.' The coldly blazing sapphire eyes regarded her narrowly. 'I'll talk to you in my study.'

'I'll come with you,' Barbra offered, but Julian dismissed her.

'Thank you, Barbra, I'll talk to *Miss Chantrill* alone.'

Barbra gazed after them, infuriated by the sound of a closed door. 'Damn!' she muttered violently. Why, oh why, had this happened?

Inside Julian's study the atmosphere was so chilly that Liane shivered.

'Sit down before you fall down,' Julian said curtly.

'Have you heard anything at all, Julian?' she asked him.

'Hasn't Mossleigh been able to help you?'

'Please, don't start about Sir Eric. Not again.'

'How old are you now, lady?' he asked raspingly. 'Twenty-six isn't it? About time you stopped acting the dewy innocent, don't you think?'

'Just a glass of water, Julian,' she whispered, bending her shining head.

'Take this.' He stood above her, a frown furrowing the area between his winged black brows. 'Take it, I said.'

She accepted the crystal tumbler from him, draining the fiery contents to give her strength. She was always vulnerable to him; his harshness was searing her skin.

'We've worked out a plan,' he told her abruptly, resting his tall lean frame against the desk.

'Can you tell me?' She plucked up her courage.

'No, I can't. You might run and tell Mossleigh, then we'll have it splashed over one of his newspapers.'

'You can't believe that,' she whispered, looking into his eye.

'Why not?' Furiously he swung away from her. 'I know nothing about you.'

'You know I love Jonathon,' she said in a grave voice.

'Of course you do. That's why you left him.'

'I left *you*.'

'Hell, yes.' He turned on her, giving a menacing laugh. 'You couldn't possibly wait to get the divorce over and done with. Mossleigh gave you tremendous support. Fitted you up with a job. How come he hasn't got around to proposing marriage yet?'

'I am certain it has never crossed his mind.'

His expression as he looked down at her was hard and uncompromising. 'I don't know which is the greater evil, stupidity or blindness. Mossleigh wanted you from the first moment. I was fool enough to allow you two to meet. He's a man long used to getting his way.'

'Perhaps he is,' Liane said bleakly, 'but he's old enough to be my father.'

'God in Heaven!' he cried aloud. 'Women marry much older men every day. Isn't that what a beautiful woman is all about? Becoming the proud possession of a rich man?'

'It might be for some. Never for me.'

'So you're not a success at anything?'

'I leave all the success to you. I didn't come here to hurt you, Julian.'

'My lady, you couldn't!' His fine nostrils flared and his blue eyes burned.

'Is there something I could do?' she begged. 'It's unbearable waiting at home.'

'Surely Mossleigh offered you his support?' His deep-timbred voice was laced with contempt. 'I simply cannot accept that he didn't. I have my spies too, Miss Chantrill.'

'I believe it.' She swallowed. 'Sir Eric means nothing to me, Julian.'

'Little fool!' he said explosively. 'When he's ready to move he will. But I'll be there. I'm always there.'

'But you don't care for me!'

'What once was mine is always mine, Liane,' he returned savagely. Where once the chiselled severity was tempered with tenderness and his flashing smile, now he looked as cold and unyielding as steel. A handsome, powerful, implacable man.

'Then you can tell me nothing?' Her eyes were brilliant with unshed tears.

'You look exhausted,' he countered shortly. 'Perhaps it's best you came to me. As it was, I was arranging to have you brought here.'

'Why?' she asked startled.

'Why?' His eyes scorched her. 'Because you're my wife.'

'Your ex-wife.'

'A lot of people still call you Mrs Wilde. I happen to be one of them. I'm not a great believer in divorce. We don't know who these people are who took Jonathon, but we're working on it. Very fast. The reliable word off the streets is no respectable member of the underworld would touch it. Kidnapping, even among criminals, is a heinous crime. Inspector Roland and I feel we're dealing with a ring-in. Someone stupid, desperate or both. Someone looking for some quick money.'

'But you can pay it.' Liane's gentle voice was husky with urgency.

'Of course.' There was murder in his eyes. 'Only we have to wait for when and where.'

'Oh, Julian!' She felt such a surge of grief that she wrapped her slender arms around her body.

For an instant it looked as if he were going to comfort her, instead he picked up a book and thumped it violently between his hands. 'Who would do this to me. Who?'

Liane closed her eyes, and when she opened them she seemed to see someone looking in at her from the glass. 'Didn't you have someone from some agency when Mrs Michaels was ill?' she asked spontaneously.

Julian turned back and stared at her. 'What?'

'I'm grasping at straws. Surely the police have asked if there were any changes in the household?'

'Of course.' His voice was harshly clipped. 'That was almost a year ago and only then for a couple of days. God, why should it slip my mind?'

'Because you're so busy. Did anyone actually check if the agency sent her?'

'Mrs Michaels, I imagine.' Julian's voice had a discernible trace of hope in it.

'She was ill.'

'Barbra, then. My God, let's get Barbra in here. Better still, we'll go back to the library. Inspector Roland should hear this.'

'It probably means nothing,' Liane wavered. 'Maybe I'm maligning some totally innocent person.'

'No one innocent has to worry.' Julian almost lifted her from her chair, and as he did so the familiar thrill of electricity ran through Liane's icy veins, warming them to urgent life. 'Let's go back into the other room. I barely laid eyes on that woman. Perhaps once or twice.'

In the library Barbra bitterly protested that she had had no cause to check out the temporary help's credentials. Mrs Michaels had only been laid up a few days, in any case, and they had dealt with the same agency many times before.

Mrs Michaels, when summoned, showed the same agitation. All she recalled of the woman, Mrs Ethel Portman, was that she was very quiet but efficient. The sort of woman whom one scarcely noticed but who gave no cause for complaint.

'I'm quite certain it couldn't possibly be her, Mr Wilde,' Mrs Michaels declared apprehensively. 'The agency people are always thoroughly checked out.'

'By whom?'

'Why, the agency,' Mrs Michaels replied.

'Did anyone visit her here?' Julian asked.

'You know I wouldn't allow anything like that,' Mrs Michaels replied, horrified. 'The only person I ever saw with her was her son. A nice young fellow. He used to pick her up in the evening.'

'You never thought to tell us this before?' Barbra challenged, sounding furious.

'How could I, Miss Edwards?' Mrs Michaels blanched. 'I never thought of it.'

'I always thought you were an intelligent woman.'

'That will do, Mrs Michaels,' Julian said dismissively. 'You should know I don't blame you. I never thought of the woman myself. My wife did that.'

Barbra's expression was thunderstruck. Her eyes went to Liane, the intensity of her gaze disturbing. 'Julian appears to have forgotten you two are divorced. I suppose the shock explains it.'

'Right!' Inspector Roland, a stocky, almost genial-looking man interrupted crisply. 'It should be easy enough to check out this Mrs Portman.'

Julian turned his raven head swiftly. 'You're to stay here, Liane.'

'She can come home with me.' Barbra moved over and put an arm around Liane's shoulder.

'I don't want her anywhere else but *here*.'

'Very well, Julian.' Barbra gave an embarrassed little laugh at the severity of his tone. 'You won't mind if I stay myself? I'm shaking so much I don't think I should drive.'

'Please yourself, Barbra,' Julian nodded shortly. 'Now take yourself off while we make a few phone calls. I can't help thinking this Mrs Portman has more to tell us.'

# CHAPTER TWO

AROUND three o'clock in the morning Liane sat bolt upright in her strange bed. She must have drifted off, though she had been lying sleepless until well after one, and the soft blue lamps on the bedside tables either side of the bed were still on.

She slipped out of bed, her heart pounding. She had assumed some noise had woken her up, but the big house was silent. She was wearing her satin slip as a nightdress, and now she slipped on the short midnight blue robe Julian had thrown across the bed without a word. She had remained in the house to appease him, and she and Barbra had passed the long anxious hours together, Barbra retiring shortly after midnight when it seemed unlikely Julian would return home. He had followed Inspector Roland back to the city headquarters and they had heard nothing from him since. Only Sir Eric had rung, illustrating the reliability of his sources, privately furious Liane had allowed Wilde to dictate to her.

Liane went to the tall, arched bay windows and looked out. The grounds were bathed in a white, radiant moonlight and for some reason her heart lifted, the terrible press of fear and anxiety inexplicably falling away. Hers was a very sensitive nature, and she found herself crossing herself as though her ceaseless prayers had been answered. Finally she opened the window, and just as she did so, powerful car lights beamed across the huge front gates.

Julian! She recognised the distinctive bulk of the Mercedes. Another moment while he operated the remote-control, then the car was gliding up the drive, coming to a halt at the base of the stairs. Liane hung dangerously out of the window and stared down. Shivers rocked her, but inside her was a tremendous hope. Julian stepped out on to the gravel, then went around to the passenger seat which from Liane's angle reclined out of sight.

She gripped her hands on the window-ledge as she realised Julian had someone with him. A small figure he was lifting out in his arms. Oh Julian, I love you, she called from her heart. I've always loved you and I always shall!

She didn't stop to think. She rushed out of the bedroom along the wide dimly lit corridor and down the great curving stairway. Tears overflowed her eyes, but she made no attempt to stop them. Jonathon had been rescued. She felt Julian's boundless relief. *His* fear was *her* fear now that Julian held his small son in his arms.

Moonlight rayed through the tall glassed archways. Liane unbolted the door, nearly throwing herself off her feet in her haste, and ran out on to the terrace.

She stared down at Julian, who paused for a moment staring up at her.

'You have him. Dear God, you have him!' Her voice was urgent, shaking. She ran to him and fell against his tall powerful figure, sobbing.

'We're out of the nightmare,' he said emotionally, swamped by his own feelings. 'What they started, I finished.'

'He's all right, isn't he?' Liane dashed her hand across her wet cheeks, staring down at the small, peacefully sleeping figure.

'He's drugged. They put him under some pretty strong sedation right from the beginning.'

'It was that woman?' Liane marvelled, clinging in high relief to Julian's arm.

'The son was the real villain,' he told her grimly. 'He forced her into it. On drugs. Out of work. They planned to get the money and head north. It was as well the mother was involved. Jonathon wasn't hurt. She swore they meant him no harm. Nevertheless, they will pay!'

'I'll cherish this night,' Liane said fervently, resting her blonde head against his shoulder.

'Will you?' He looked down at her, the bitterness creeping back in.

'You know I love Jonathon.'

'But you left him.' Julian walked on and Liane followed him up.

'I'll turn down his bed. Which room is it? I couldn't bear to ask before.'

'Beside mine,' Julian told her briefly, pausing while she reset the locks on the door. 'Turn right at the top of the stairs. It connects with my room. I'll be there should he wake up.'

'Of course.' Overcome, she lifted Jonathon's small fingers and kissed them.

The master suite was huge, with a connecting sitting-room between it and Jonathon's bedroom. Julian indicated the lighting panel and Liane flicked a few switches.

'Leave those,' he told her. 'They're all we need.'

As it happened, only lamps on wall brackets came on in the master suite, gilding the panelled walls and a remarkable coffered ceiling. Liane ran to Jonathon's room and folded back the covers on the bed. She plumped up the pillows and looked back at Julian, who lowered his son carefully on to the patterned sheet. He was still in his school uniform, and Liane bit hard on her lip so that she wouldn't start crying again.

Tenderly she released Jonathon's tie and opened up the buttons of his white shirt. He was sleeping so heavily that she risked lifting him so that she could slip it off.

Next came his shoes and long socks, the grey flannel shorts. Finally she folded the top sheet over him and bent down and kissed his rounded forehead. He was a remarkably handsome little boy, the mirror image of his father.

'This must never happen again,' she said as they moved back into the adjoining room.

'It won't,' Julian said quietly. 'I'll have to involve myself in every single thing that goes on. If you hadn't remembered that woman, it might have taken days for someone else to. I've left so much to my staff. Mrs Michaels is a good woman, but none of us has been careful enough.'

'They had him in the city?'

'In a farmhouse thirty miles from here. A place called Cowley's Crossing. We surrounded the place and I went in. They barely put up a struggle. Just as well: we all have a capacity for violence. As it was, I left that particular bit of scum feeling very sorry for himself.'

'I wonder what state Jonathon will be in when he wakes up,' Liane said urgently. 'It must have been a frightening experience for him. He's so intelligent, he must have known at once someone was taking him out of his father's custody.'

Julian came to stand beside her, staring down at his son. 'If anything had happened to Jonathon...'

'Don't!'

'I haven't been coping all that well with you gone.'

Liane was confused. 'That's hard to believe, Julian. You haven't been lonely all this time.'

'You're convinced of that, are you?'

She avoided his mesmeric eyes. 'I expect I can sleep now.'

'Don't tell me you've forgotten what it was like to sleep with me?'

'On *my* part it was an act of love,' she said, not bothering to hide her emotion.

'And me?' He suddenly grasped her by the upper arms and turned her to face him. 'What was I supposed to be doing, slaking some insatiable lust?'

'Julian, you're hurting me.' She extended her slender fingers.

'I don't *want* to hurt you,' he said savagely, 'I want to thank you.'

'No, don't.' Blue fire washed over her, stunning sensation.

'Why not? There's no woman in the world I'd rather make love to than you.' He swept her into his arms, forcing her head back into the crook of his shoulder. He held her. Locked her in his arms. 'Liane. Sweet Liane,' he murmured in bitter mockery.

She couldn't move. Couldn't turn her head. Her eyelids were weighed, her mouth parting, so with a violent exclamation his plunged over it, catching up the edges of her full, tender lips. Inside her heart began to wail even as her body reacted excitedly. Julian's touch had always been like quickfire. Past and present fused for a moment. She was possessed by the old desire, so even as his hand ran fiercely over her body and finally claimed her naked breast she couldn't break away from him.

Passion and pain were simultaneous. She was no longer his wife. He was *violating* her, yet she allowed him to put his mouth to her breast, drawing on the tautly aroused nipple, and a searingly sweet pain like a knife ran from her breast to her womb. His robe fell from her. He was peeling the satin slip from her body, her skin in the lamplight having the luminosity of a pearl.

'I *want* you,' he whispered harshly. 'I want you every time I wake up in the night.'

'Julian.' As she forced open her drugged eyes she caught sight of the two of them reflected in the tall standing pierglass. Their images looked incredibly erotic, something from an allegorical painting; she all white and gold against Julian's brutal unrelieved black. It was beautiful and it was frightening, a monument to love...or to lust.

'This is wrong, Julian!' she cried angrily.

'Is it? I don't particularly care. To me it's the most natural thing in the world.'

'I don't want this.'

'You will.' He caressed her voluptuously with strong hands that were faintly trembling. 'I'm not going to rape you, Liane.' His beautiful mouth twisted crookedly.

'It seems that way.' His eyes on her body were even worse than his hands. She was terribly torn. She wanted this to happen, yet she was frantic to break away. 'Do you really think you only have to snap your fingers and I'll submit?'

'I think after all I do want to hurt you,' he said cuttingly. 'Rouse you. Then push you away.'

'I'll never understand you.' She threw back her white-gold head.

'No.'

'I want my robe, Julian.'

'Let me.' He laughed without humour. 'Naked, you're as beautiful as a lily.' He ran his hands down her slender back, moved them back to span her narrow waist. 'If only beauty alone could make a man entirely happy. What about trust, loyalty?'

'*You* couldn't want to talk about that,' she said shakily. 'Please let me put the robe on.'

'You look better without it, but if you insist. It goes over your shoulders and you tuck your arms in it.' He dressed her like a child, and she had to allow him to because there was a menace behind the pseudo gentleness. Finally he flipped her long blonde hair out over the rolled collar. 'Why look so tortured? Remember how I used to call you my mermaid with your hair all brushed out? I loved you in those long shimmering things you used to wear for bed. I can still hear the faint static as I pulled them off.'

'It's late Julian.'

'A quick kiss goodnight?'

'You're a cruel devil, aren't you?'

'If I am, you made me.' His tone was forceful and, to her surprise, starkly sincere.

'Adulterer.' The word was torn out of her as she relived her stormy suffering.

'Idiot child! Have you ever bothered to find out what *really* happened two years ago?'

'Tell me about it,' she cried. 'I'd *adore* to hear it all over again.'

'Only now, as then, you'd refuse to listen.'

'*Listen!*' Her breasts rose and fell with her rapid breathing. 'I hate you for what you did to me, Julian.'

'Hate. Did you hate me just now?' His blue eyes blazed. 'Another moment and I would have had you.'

'Thank God we're apart.' She began trembling uncontrollably, and just at that moment a little whimper sliced into their private war and instantly both of them returned to the bed. Jonathon was moving restlessly, his short black curls damp against his temples, his satiny cheeks rosy.

'Hush, darling.' Liane moved across the bed, half lying beside him, stroking his head. 'Hush, my beloved boy.' She continued her gentle stroking until Jonathon's whimpers subsided and he visibly relaxed.

'He always was silly about you,' Julian said bitterly. 'You were the princess from a fairy-tale, all long pale golden hair and jewel eyes. Too young to be a mother.

Jonathon's marvellous playmate. He loved you. My stupid, obdurate, pampered little wife.'

'It doesn't matter. None of it matters,' Liane said without expression. 'All we have in common is Jonathon.'

'Go to hell, Liane,' he said violently. 'You've put me there.'

Even in a deep sleep Jonathon heard their voices. He mumbled something aloud, then momentarily opened his eyes.

As it happened his gaze fell on Liane, her lovely face tender between the shining curtains of her ash-gold hair. The last time he had seen her he had been four years of age. Little more than a baby. They had been together two years and those two years had been wonderful. Still, children forget.

'Lee!' he said sweetly as though they had never parted.

'I'm here, darling.' She bent and kissed him quickly.

'His memory is excellent. Like mine.'

'He hasn't forgotten me,' Liane said shakily, though once more Jonathon's blue eyes had closed.

'He's as mixed-up as I am.'

Liane looked up at Julian's tall, dominating figure standing beside the bed. 'Did you allow him to have my presents?'

'What presents?'

'The presents that I sent him. Christmas, Easter, his birthday, without fail.'

'Except they never arrived. Poor packaging, I suppose.'

'Ask Barbra,' Liane's voice sounded shocked. 'Barbra always delivered them for me.'

'When you were a little girl did you always tell lies?'

'I've never lied in my life. Not about anything even vaguely important.'

'Little white lies, perhaps?' Julian turned away, his striking face contemptuous. 'You have a powerful weapon over me. My son loves you. Moreover, I am deeply in your debt. You are wholly responsible for his swift recovery. Eventually we would have come up with that woman's name, but my little son would have had to wait. I can never repay you.'

Liane slipped off the bed and went to him, although his expression was dark and alien. 'I don't think payment of any kind has ever been in my mind.'

His blue eyes seared her. 'You don't have to remind me of your stubborn pride. As my wife...'

'Ex-wife.'

'...you were entitled to a handsome settlement. I was rich enough to give it to you and not miss it.'

'All I wanted from you, Julian,' Liane said bleakly, 'was your love.'

'Forgive me if I'm puzzled that you thought you never had it. I thought I brought you everything I was.'

'Except I couldn't adapt to it. Your capacities, Julian, are far beyond the norm. I couldn't adapt to a life where I felt worthless.'

'My God,' he exploded violently, 'such a reaction to a vicious lie.'

Liane shook her pale gold head. 'I don't want to talk about it. Not any more. My physical feeling for you may still be intense, but there's a profound difference between us. I would never betray you.'

'Only with a man old enough to be your father.'

'You don't mean that. You *can't* mean that.' Liane's sea-coloured eyes reflected her shock.

'Oh, Liane, but I do.' He suddenly reached out and gripped her delicate shoulders. 'If you think you've been through a terrible trauma, try getting involved with that swine Mossleigh.'

He was holding her so powerfully she knew there would be bruises. 'Sir Eric is a highly respected man.'

'Sir Eric is a schizophrenic,' he chopped her off. 'You don't need a master's degree in psychology to figure that. He operates on two levels. One is the highly respected businessman, the philanthropist, the other is the knowing instigator of many a man's downfall.'

'Which, of course, you're not!' Liane said very carefully, for the tears in her throat. 'Tony Bannigan didn't have a chance against you.'

'I was his enemy then. Not now. Bannigan never knew anything about his wife's running around.'

'What, to you?'

'What sort of a fool are you?' Julian looked at her intensely. 'You spent every night of your life in my arms. We were talking about starting a family because we wanted *our* child so badly. A brother or sister for Jonathon. At the best time of my life, the most rhapsodic of our marriage, I was spending my spare time with another woman? A woman, moreover, who had absolutely no appeal for me?'

'Not to hear her talk,' Liane said sadly. 'Please, must we go over this? I've shut the gates on that part of my life. It was beautiful and dangerous and killing.'

'But we never *talked*. You would never listen.' He was looking down at her with contemptuous intensity.

'I couldn't then and I can't now. Not to this very night. *Please*, Julian. I can't seem to stop shaking. I've cried myself to sleep more nights than I can count but I swore I'd never do it any more. You exposed my heart, my very essence. You were in my bloodstream. With no one else could I ever share such intimacies. I worshipped you all right. You weren't only the most wonderful sexual partner a woman could ever want, you were everything: my dearest, closest friend and companion, even the father I lost. There's been no person in the world I loved as much as you. Can't you understand how I felt when you betrayed me? There's no other word. I lost my anchor in life. All security. It's taken two years to find a certain degree of peace. I've always been profoundly frightened of seeing you again.'

'Yet you came.'

'I felt you were calling to me. Surely I was crazy, but I thought you needed me. I thought Jonathon was calling to me from a distance. I swear I don't know how that woman, that temporary housekeeper flashed into my head. Barbra only told me about her once. I've always had a strange ability to sense danger.'

'I expect it goes with erratic behaviour.' The steely pressure relented and wearily Julian dropped his hands. 'Go to bed, Liane. It's almost dawn. We can't discuss anything now. You're wrong, in any case. I *don't* need you. I don't need any woman. God help me if I did. I can't say that of Jonathon yet. He's just a child.

From long habit Liane woke at seven, and because she was in a strange house she resisted her tiredness and got up to shower and dress. The room she occupied was cool, fresh, blue and white, the custom-made carpet geometric in design, working surprisingly well with the floral pattern of the curtains and the upholstery on the daybed and two armchairs. The quilted bedspread was a glossy white. Paintings hung on the wall and there was a tall, beautiful bouquet of spring flowers on the Regency table set before the bay windows. A splendidly appointed bathroom adjoined, stocked with expensive toiletries and a collection of fluffy blue towels in all sizes. Luxuriant ferns stood before the tall stained-glass window, revelling in the light and humidity. It was a woman's suite, Liane concluded with very little brain-power. There were fragrant soaps, bath-salts, talcs and body lotions, everything a guest could want. The only thing that surprised her was there wasn't a collection of women's cosmetics, Estée Lauder or perhaps Lancôme. Women were important to Julian, even if only to give him pleasure.

She looked rather pale, with faint shadows beneath her eyes. A light application of foundation soon fixed that, and she applied a little blusher just under her cheekbones. There, she looked better. Much better. Make-up, however light, was an armour. She always carried a small stock of it in a cosmetic bag that fitted neatly into her handbag. Today her eyes were more blue than green, and she supposed it was the reflected light. Strange how her eyes were so changeable. Julian *had* always called her his mermaid. She hadn't expected him to remember that. His feeling for her, after all, hadn't been very profound. He was easily moved to physical passion. Their marriage had been biological.

And what of little Jonathon? How quickly would he throw off his trauma? His experience would have pushed his natural bravery to the limit. He could have fought them, resisted, or had they drugged him immediately? Such an abrupt curtailing of his personal liberty would have changed his world. She was immensely grateful he so clearly remembered her. Her face had comforted him immediately he had opened his eyes. She knew he had understood he was safe. Her feeling for him was still extremely intense, as it was for his father. She could never break away. Never close them off. How extraordinary that Julian should deny they had received her gifts. Or was it simply another form of rejection? His words gave her the feeling she was moving through a hazy world where nothing was truly real. She would have to tread very carefully.

She was barely dressed when someone knocked on her door, then pushed it open without waiting for permission.

Barbra burst in, her tall, ultra-slim figure wrapped in a gorgeous Ming-blue kimono almost the colour of Julian's eyes. She spoke excitedly, with more amazement than gratitude.

'The boy's back!'

Liane could not conceal a powerful surge of distaste. '*Jonathon* is home.'

'That's what I said.' Barbra vigorously nodded her dark head. 'I can't believe it, can you?'

'It does seem like a miracle.' Liane half turned her back to her. Why was Barbra so different?

'You don't seem surprised.' Barbra rushed to the bay window so that she could face Liane.

'I was there when Julian brought him back home.'

'And when was this?' Barbra's eyes flashed.

'A few minutes after three this morning.'

'Do put down that brush, Liane,' Barbra exhorted her. 'I must speak to you.' The sight of Liane's beautiful hair unrestrained appeared to be annoying her. 'Julian and Dr Morrison are with the boy now.'

'Can't you say Jonathon?' Liane asked quietly.

'Jonathon, the boy, what does it matter? You are being difficult this morning, Liane.'

'Who told you?' Liane asked, confining her long hair at the nape of her neck.

'Mrs Michaels. She couldn't wait. She woke me up. I'd taken two sleeping-pills, so you can imagine how I felt.'

'Sublimely grateful, I would have thought.'

'Of course I was,' Barbra confirmed very quickly. 'Don't misunderstand me, Liane. Jonathon is my nephew. My dead sister's only child. Even now I can't believe she's gone.'

'Yes, I know. I understand tragedy, Barbra.'

'He adored her. I don't think he has ever come to terms with what happened.'

'I imagine not. Our loved ones live on in our memory.'

Barbra's dark eyes were now studying the dressing-table. 'You've still got the pearls.'

'They were my wedding present, after all.'

'I thought you gave back everything.' Barbra seemed to move under a great compulsion. She picked up the lustrous strand and without permission slipped them around her neck, adjusting the exquisite diamond clasp so that it fell below her collarbone. 'They're magnificent, aren't they?' She bent slightly so that she could look into the oval mirror.

'Beautiful,' Liane agreed, trying to control an impulse to tell Barbra to take them off.

'I can't remember Caroline getting anything as fabulous as this. Then, of course, Julian wasn't where he is now. His rise has been phenomenal, especially when you consider Jonathon Wilde, the father, was wiped out. I remember Father was none too happy about Julian. He was positive he would go the same way as his father.'

'Yet it didn't stop you and your sister.' The words surged so spontaneously they almost stopped Liane's breath.

Barbra stopped her preening and faced her. 'What in the world are you talking about?' There was anger in the dark eyes.

Liane was silent for a moment then she said, 'Someone told me both you and Caroline were interested in Julian.'

'My dear girl, that's utter nonsense.'

'Is it?' Liane faced her, her blue-green eyes very clear and direct.

'It most certainly is!' Barbra looked shocked. 'We've been friends for years, Liane. Now this! May I ask who told you?'

'Sir Eric Mossleigh.' Liane leaned forward to pick up her gold watch.

'Well, he would, wouldn't he?' Barbra shrugged her straight shoulders.

'To what purpose?'

Barbra laughed a little. 'Liane, whenever are you going to grow up?'

'I'll have to, that's clear. You're denying it?'

'Good God, Liane! I expected better of you.'

'Do you deny not passing on my gifts to Jonathon?'

'Oh, that.' Barbra swung away. 'I didn't intend to tell you. I didn't want to hurt you any more than you have been. Julian wanted to wipe you out. Your memory. Everything. I'm sure you'll agree, Julian is not a man to trifle with.'

'The presents were for *Jonathon*,' Liane pointed out with a profound sense of having been deceived.

Barbra studied her very earnestly. 'My dear, please try to see it from my side. You brought chaos into Julian's life. As much as I like and admire you, I knew from the beginning that the marriage wouldn't work. You were too young. You still are. You're a babe in the wood, and Julian was the ravening wolf. Your beauty snared him. For a while. If you want to understand Julian you have to understand once he's got something he moves on. Lesley Bannigan wasn't important, but she knew how to play the game. There were others. Julian is a spectacular man. Women chase him in droves. Is it any wonder he hasn't learnt fidelity?'

'We were talking about Jonathon.' Liane spoke with a bluntness that apprently stunned the older woman. 'Why was it you never passed on my presents?'

'I did not wish to invite Julian's anger. Surely you can see that? I am family. I had to tread very carefully. I do not take sides, but in risking Julian's anger I could have been cut off from my nephew.'

'I didn't think you liked children.'

Barbra gave a short, unhappy laugh. She pressed her hand to her heart. 'Liane, whatever has got into you?'

'Maybe a veil has dropped from my eyes. I trusted you, Barbra. Really trusted you.'

'So what has happened then to change it?' Barbra asked in amazement. 'Didn't I help you through the days of your marriage? Wasn't I always there to support and advise? I'm deeply sorry I didn't tell you about the presents, but you must believe I was acting with the best possible motives. I was trying to help you through a most difficult time. Divorce involves a lot of unhappiness, and what deeper humiliation is there for a woman than to be cast aside?'

'*I* started divorce proceedings, Barbra,' Liane pointed out, her voice very disciplined.

'Of course you did. But what else could you do?'

Liane shook her pale-gold head. 'I could have taken my time. I see that now. I'm older. I've more experience to draw on. You're right. I was a babe in the wood and I reacted like a desolate child.'

'My dear,' Barbra laughed shortly, her attractive face sardonic. 'I hope you're not going to see Julian as a man wronged. He had many women. Not just Lesley Bannigan. Could you really face that sort of life?'

'Lesley Bannigan was a friend of yours, wasn't she?'

Barbra's clear-skinned face set in lines of strain. 'Lesley Bannigan was a long-time acquaintance. There is a huge difference. I don't quite see what you're implying.'

'Both of you were almost ten years older. Maybe I should be seeing myself as the victim. Do you realise I never had a moment's doubt about Julian? Although our life was absolutely perfect, I believed at once he had deceived me. That shows at once a lack of trust. A lack of maturity.'

'Darling,' Barbra moaned, 'please don't start with your lost hopes and dreams. The point is, Julian did betray you and you had two options. Either to turn a blind eye, which, my dear, many women do. Or, proceed with a divorce. One acts according to one's nature. I could never see *you* as a promiscuous person.'

'Yet you've always insisted that is Julian's normal mode of behaviour.'

'Are you doubting he isn't out with beautiful women all the time?'

'As far as anyone knows he isn't doing anything. He's photographed with them.'

'My dear, you really do need massive evidence, don't you?'

'Maybe now, when my life is beyond repair.'

'Then you must still love him.' Barbra's finely cut lips twisted.

'I don't know what my feelings for Julian are.' Liane evaded the point.

'Well, I can tell you what his feelings are for you.' Barbra's voice sounded strong and protective. 'He sees you as a sex object he can pick up and set aside. Why do you think I'm not married? I place pride and independence before anything else. Like you, I couldn't exist in a married situation where the husband was unfaithful. My nature cannot share. Infidelity, for the injured party, must be a frightful experience. When it comes to sex, men are different. That goes without saying. We women are so terribly, terribly vulnerable. I admire you tremendously for turning the tables on Julian. I believe he thought because you were so young he could turn you into anything he wanted. He's such a demanding man. We women know love is much, much more than sexual desire. You'll find a good man to live with. A real man.'

'And Julian's not real?' Liane asked ironically.

'You know what I *mean* dear. A man who wants a *real* relationship. Julian is married to the High Priestess,

Big Business. He gets his real thrills out of amassing a great fortune.'

'No.' Liane shook her head. 'I've come to believe Julian made some commitment to his father. Strange as it sounds, I think that drives him.'

'That and a need to smash your boss,' Barbra pointed out acidly. 'Of course that comes from Mossleigh's paying *you* some attention. It's no secret you enchanted him on sight. Some men do fall madly in love in middle age. They find some highly desirable female to keep them young. I can't help wondering if Sir Eric mightn't be your best bet. He could give you a wonderful life.'

'Sir Eric's behaviour towards me is and always has been impeccable,' Liane answered coolly though she felt sick inside. 'I am his employee. His secretary.'

'Now listen to the child!' Barbra laughed. 'My dear, Sir Eric Mossleigh was smitten with you from the moment he laid eyes on you. Don't forget I was there. Nobody has to tell me about these things. I know. Don't look so offended. He's a wonderful man. You could make things very easy for yourself if you gave him the slightest encouragement.'

Liane was aghast. 'Obviously you've forgotten he's old enough to be my father.'

'Listen to your head, dear. Not your heart.' Barbra glanced at her pityingly. 'What a woman really needs is security. I promise you you would blossom if you were married to a man like Eric Mossleigh.'

'Thank you, but that's completely out of the question. Not only has he never acted out of character, but I feel nothing for him but respect.'

Barbra smiled. 'I would have thought respect a great start.'

'Please drop this line of talk, Barbra. I find it distasteful.'

'You'll never learn, will you?' Barbra asked. 'You're not a young woman any more. You should be careful. In a few years' time you'll be thirty. A little more time after that and you'll have silver hairs in among the gold. With your bones I don't mean you'll be anything else but beautiful, but you won't be *young*. Youth is what all men desire. A woman's ambitions are tied to her beauty. You could bring a great deal to the right marriage. You have everything going for you. Don't let some girlish quibbling ruin your chances. Eric Mossleigh is a handsome man. In the prime of life. He's one of the richest men in the country and a most cultivated man. A pity you're not more in tune with reality. I could name any number of women in this city who'd give their eye-teeth to be in your position. How can you be so foolish? If you had any doubts let me assure you Eric Mossleigh worships the ground you tread on. He sees himself as your great protector. He's a wonderfully acceptable and attractive man. Why don't you give him a chance?'

'I must be peculiar,' Liane said. 'I could never marry a man I didn't love.'

'Well, you did that and it didn't work out at all.' Barbra gave a little deprecating laugh. 'Is it so hard to imagine yourself as Lady Mossleigh?'

Liane's beautiful eyes clouded. 'Not only hard, impossible. How subtly you've always worked to influence me.'

'Surely that makes me a real friend? I really care about you, Liane. You need somebody to help you through this. You have no family. I like to think I've filled some gap.'

Liane went to the bay windows and looked out. 'That's the doctor leaving. I must go to Jonathon.' She drew a short, shallow breath. 'It will be remarkable if he comes out of this without any ill effects.'

'I'll have to work very hard to see that he does,' Barbra returned in a low, moving voice. 'I'm committed to my sister's son. You said you were up when Julian brought him back. How was that?'

'Unlike you, I didn't take sleeping-pills,' Liane observed wryly. 'I was saying my prayers and I must have drifted off. Something woke me just as Julian drove up to the gates. Some recognition, some deep knowledge that Jonathon was safe. Do you suppose it was because of our deep bond?'

'Certainly, my dear. You were friends.'

'More than friends, Barbra.' Liane turned to face her, sunlight transforming her hair to living gold. 'Jonathon really did love me, and I love him.'

'So where does this take you, my dear?' Barbra looked up with sympathy in her eyes. 'Julian and you might be able to talk civilly at this particular point of time, but given a day or two everything will return to normal.'

'Oh, I do hope so!' Liane exclaimed feelingly. 'Our only hope is that Jonathon will take this as some kind of adventure. He wasn't hurt. It would be sad if he were to become anxious.'

'Leave it to me, Liane,' Barbra said bracingly, getting to her feet. 'Jonathon is very much like his father. I see none of my family in him at all. My sister gave him birth yet he's all Wilde. Extraordinary, isn't it? Yet his toughness should get him through his ordeal. You're not going to work?'

'No. Sir Eric wouldn't hear of it. He saw how upset I was. I'm hoping to stay with Jonathon for the rest of the day.'

'Have you asked Julian?' Barbra's thin black brows rose in amazement.

'I don't think he will have any objection. Julian only wants what is best for his son.'

'You're absolutely selfless, aren't, you, Liane? Such a dear girl.' Barbra moved gracefully towards the door. 'Of course, I'll have to think about moving in. At least for a while. Perhaps three or four months. Julian has asked me before. I don't think he realises how *much* he depends on me.'

'Oh, Barbra...'

'Yes, dear.' Barbra swung to face her, one hand on the door-knob.

'Do you think I could have my pearls?'

## CHAPTER THREE

THE DOOR of Julian's room was open when Liane tapped on it. Julian was sitting on the bed, his back to her, his wide shoulders almost hiding his small son from sight.

'May I come in?'

'You're asking permission?' Julian stood up at once, smiling tightly, and Jonathon called from the bed.

'Lee, oh, Lee!' He threw out his arms with a soft look of wonder and Liane went to him, gathering him into an emotional embrace.

'How's my boy?'

Jonathon was breathing deeply into her throat. 'I *knew* you were real.'

'I'm real, darling. I'm here.' Liane bent her head protectively over him, feeling the quivers in his small, sturdy body.

'A bad man took me away.'

'Yes, and Daddy brought you home.' Liane's voice was husky. 'Daddy would never let anything happen to you.'

'I cried for you.'

'Did you, darling?'

'I've cried for you a lot.'

'Well, I'm here now.'

'And you'll never go away?' Liane's distressed eyes flew to Julian's face. 'I want you to stay here and take care of me.'

'I'm here, darling,' Liane soothed him.

Jonathon shifted his position and sat back, staring up at her. 'You will, you really will?' His flower-blue eyes glowed.

'What, darling?' Liane swallowed on the hard lump in her throat.

'Stay with me. Daddy said I can have a dog. Not a little dog either. A big dog. They call them German shepherds.'

'Well, they make wonderful guardians and companions.'

Jonathon reached out a tentative hand and touched Liane's hair. She sat still and he pulled at the clasp so that her hair flowed forward in a shining curtain. 'I recognised you last night.' He smiled at her.

'Of course you did. You're my boy and you know it.'

'Why did you go away?' He looked at her with a quizzical, deeply hurt expression.

'I told you, Jonathon,' Julian said. 'Liane and I separated.'

'The kids in my class said you were divorced.'

'We are divorced, Jonathon,' Liane said. 'But that doesn't mean things have changed for you and me. I'll always love you.'

'I'm six.'

'I know. You've grown tall.'

'Why didn't you come and see me?'

Liane felt stricken, weak. 'I thought you might have forgotten me.'

'I didn't. I look at you all the time. In my old storybook.'

'And how do you feel this morning?' Liane asked, looking back at him lovingly.

'Dr Morrison has been here,' Jonathon said importantly. 'He said I'm going like a little train.'

'Well, that's great.' She gave him her sweet, luminous smile. 'What would you like to do today?'

'Go on a picnic with you and Daddy. Like we used to. Better still, I want to go to the beach. Daddy thinks I can't remember Sandpiper, but I can. I remember how you used to take me swimming, even when it rained. I remember making sand-castles. What happened to all those buckets and spades?'

'I guess they're still around some place.'

'Can we go to the beach, Lee?'

'Darling...' Liane was about to say she couldn't leave her job, instead she said, 'what about school?'

'I'm not *going* to school,' Jonathon suddenly burst out in intense reaction. 'That man might be there.'

'No, Jonathon.' Liane caught his hands. 'That man will never bother you again. A policeman has taken him away. He must understand he can never do such a thing again.'

'I hit him in the nose.' Jonathon's blue eyes flared like his father's.

'And what did he do?'

'He pulled my hair. The lady gave me a lemonade to drink.'

'They didn't want to hurt you,' Liane assured him. 'They wanted Daddy to give them money for bringing you back.'

'Shows what they know,' Jonathon scoffed. 'Daddy brought me home himself.'

'We all love you very much, Jonathon,' Liane said. 'You're a strong, brave boy.'

'I am now.' Jonathon peered into her eyes. 'I was frightened before. I kept thinking Daddy wouldn't know where I was.'

'But he did! There's nowhere anyone could hide you. Daddy would find you wherever you were.'

'I think I want breakfast,' Jonathon announced. 'I suddenly feel hungry.'

'Is he allowed to get up out of bed?' Liane looked up at Julian who was watching them silently.

''Course I am now you're here.' Jonathon kicked back the bedclothes. 'Do you want to see all my toys, Lee? I think I've got hundreds since you saw me last. I'm so happy you're home.'

A few hours later as reaction caught up with him, Jonathon abruptly fell asleep. One moment he was making a model plane, the next his head slumped over on a cushion.

'Gosh, I'm tired,' he murmured as his heavy lashes dropped.

Julian carried him back to bed and Liane tucked him in. 'He seems all right,' she said gratefully. 'It's reasonable he wouldn't want to go back to school for a little while. Until the bad memory fades.'

Julian nodded, his dark face adamant. 'And that's precisely what I want to talk to you about.' He directed her into the adjoining sitting-room and shut the door carefully. 'If you want to help Jonathon, I think you could spare a few weeks out of your life.'

'What is it you have on your mind, Julian?' Her heart contracted as she allowed her gaze to fall on his tall, striking figure. He wore casual clothes, black cords with a bright blue shirt, but as ever he looked supremely elegant. She did not remember the sharp lines from nose to mouth or the severity. Julian had changed a good deal. Always powerful, with an inherent authority, his manner had hardened, become daunting.

'I should think it quite clear.' He gave her a sharp glance. 'Jonathon needs a change of scene. A glorious holiday so that he can quickly forget.'

Liane nodded. 'I agree.'

'But he wants *you*. He told you so.'

He could see the struggle in her face. 'But what about after, Julian? I would have to leave him again.'

'Let's cross that bridge when we come to it,' he told her curtly. 'You're supposed to have a heart of gold. Jonathon obviously thinks you love him. Are you telling me you're prepared to spend some little time with him?'

Liane's lovely face softened. 'I should think Sir Eric would allow it.'

'Don't talk to me about that man,' Julian flashed, his brilliant eyes menacing.

'He is my employer. I can't forget that.'

'I thought he might be your lover by now.'

'No, he isn't!' Liane said heatedly. How could anyone be, when she was supremely conscious of Julian's lean hard body only a foot away? 'I should add that Sir Eric has never treated me with anything less than courtesy and respect.'

Julian's expression was a mixture of amusement and hard contempt. 'Don't you ever see the look on the bastard's face?'

Liane flushed and her chin came up. 'You're wrong!' Her heart was pounding so loudly she was surprised he couldn't hear it.

'Do yourself a favour, *Miss Chantrill*; grow up.'

'I'm working at it,' she said shakily. 'I spoke to Barbra about Jonathon's presents. It seems she didn't pass them on because she feared your wrath.'

Julian stared at her, his gaze sharpening. 'And you counted Barbra as your friend?'

'Are you telling me she isn't?' Liane's eyes faintly misted.

Julian's mouth hardened. 'I guess I am.'

'She was always very nice to me.'

'Unhappily for you,' Julian returned enigmatically. 'You are aware I sold Sandpiper?'

'Yes. I understand it's a mistake to return to the past,' she replied emotionally. 'You can't admit wrong, Julian. You have the pride of the devil.'

'And *you don't*? Who killed our marriage? Lost two years out of our lives?' he asked with a sudden passion.

She had to take refuge from his bitterness and the turbulence in his eyes.

'Forgive me, Julian,' she said wretchedly. 'I'll speak to you another time.'

'You'll stay here.' He caught her roughly.

She threw back her head, her heightened colour emphasising the purity of her skin. 'I must say you've turned into a tyrant.'

His arousal was violent. 'There hasn't been much room in my life for lightness.'

'I will *not* be manhandled.' Even so her senses were clamouring.

'I remember when you couldn't live without my touch,' he mocked her, his sexual pull frighteningly strong.

'Too many knew your lovemaking.'

He held her even tighter, staring down into her eyes. 'Can you tell me when I found the time?'

'I can't!' She shook her head, the old griefs rising. '*Please*, Julian, if you want me to help you, to help Jonathon, you have to leave me alone.' She was almost weeping with frustration.

'I know that.' Abruptly he released her and her hand came up to rub her arm.

'Don't do that. I didn't hurt you.'

'Would you like to see?' She realised too late she was provoking him.

'Why not? I've never seen another woman with a skin like yours.' His eyes fell from her face to the low V of her silk shirt and he reached out and took the long string of pearls in his hand, warm from her body. 'Do you understand what marriage means?'

Why did he have to diminish her in her own eyes? 'Yes,' she said spiritedly. 'A solemn commitment before God.'

'So!' He looked from the pearls into her beautiful, iridescent eyes. 'Do you know I'd like to kill you?'

'Maybe I don't care.' She looked back at him defiantly.

'I swore before God I would love and cherish you until death us do part.'

She felt a terrible urge to lean forward and rest her head against his breast. Nothing he did could negate his power. 'So you were human after all.'

'If you only knew...' His black brows knotted and he was about to say more when a door slammed and a woman's high heels beat out a tattoo across an expanse of parquetry.

'That must be Barbra,' Liane said. 'It's always been surprising to me that she and Jonathon are not close.'

'Just because Jonathon is her nephew?' he asked acidly.

'Of course.' Liane's blue-green eyes were startled. 'Her own sister's child?'

'Obviously you didn't know much about the Edwards' family life. The lot of them were for ever in competition. Whatever one wanted, the other had to have it.'

'What are you saying?' She couldn't hide her bewilderment.

'Regrettably, not all sisters are good friends,' Julian said broodingly. 'Barbra has no great feeling for my son. He is *my* son, isn't he? He's the image of *me*. The ordinary family bond doesn't seem to apply.'

'I'm sure you're wrong,' Liane said earnestly. 'Barbra isn't terribly good with children, but Jonathon is her blood.'

'Spare me, sweet Liane,' he said tonelessly. 'One of the truly annoying things about Barbra is her propensity for barging in.'

The door opened and they both looked around at once. Barbra stood there, looking extremely stylish in a slim-fitting dress of black and white silk, her long neck adorned with a thick rope of eighteen-carat gold, her dark hair dressed as though she had just come from a top salon. As long as Liane had known her, Barbra never had a hair out of place, nor did she look anything less than beautifully groomed. It was a great wonder she hadn't made a brilliant marriage.

Now she arched her black brows, a certain arrogance in her dark eyes. 'I do hope I'm going to be allowed to speak to my nephew.'

Liane, in her sensitivity, flinched. 'We've been together all morning,' she offered.

'You mean you and Jonathon have been together, dear. I feel quite left out in the cold.'

Julian stared at her impassively. 'That was not the intention, Barbra. It's not surprising Jonathon has turned to Liane. She always had a special place in his life.'

'Of course.' Barbra's high-bred face relaxed into a smile. 'That's why you came, isn't it, Liane? Love drew you.'

'I must go now, however,' Liane said, uncomfortably aware of undercurrents. 'For a little while. I need clothes. I must speak to Sir Eric.'

'About what, dear?' There was surprise in Barbra's voice.

Julian answered for her. 'I've asked Liane—*Jonathon* has asked Liane to stay with him for a time. In the circumstances, I think he needs an immediate change of scene. Perhaps a few weeks at the beach. I'm sure Liane won't mind supervising his lessons. She has an arts degree, after all.'

'But really, Julian.' Barbra looked almost desperately upset. '*I'm* here. Always at your service. One of the reasons I wanted to speak to Jonathon privately was to suggest a holiday together. I know that much as you'd like to be with him, it's out of the question. All those negotiations! Without you your whole operation would very likely fall apart.'

'Are those the whispers?' Julian asked acidly.

'You know what I mean, darling!' She gave him a concerned look. 'For reasons none of us seem to understand, Liane has chosen to be a career woman and she has done remarkably well. I'm sure Eric Mossleigh would be lost without her. Isn't that right, Liane?'

'There are other secretaries,' Liane said quietly. 'Although I must admit Sir Eric has come to depend on me.'

'But then, you're special.' Barbra gave her a fond look. 'You really have the kindest heart, but I know getting time off could make things awkward for you. I'm more than happy to look after Jonathon. Surely you all realised that.'

'Except that he wants Liane,' Julian announced bluntly, looking very formidable. 'I appreciate your offer, Barbra, but it's all settled. Liane can get time off. The rest of her life, if she so chooses, and I'll organise a beach house.'

'But darling, you don't have one any more.' Barbra looked at him sharply.

'Then I'll buy one today and staff it,' he returned curtly. 'You must have forgotten, Barbra, how much money I have.'

'As if anyone could do that.' She went to him and held his arm. 'All right, your idea is even better. Liane and I get on so well together, we'll both go. Much as Liane loves Jonathon, I'm sure she doesn't want to hibernate with only a child for company. We'll be good for each other. What do you say, Liane?'

'I won't mind, Barbra.'

'I insist. I insist!' Barbra began to laugh. 'Why this is quite marvellous! Our darling boy has been returned to us and at long last there's a truce between you two. I've always hoped for it.'

Whatever qualms Liane was feeling, she mastered them. The plain fact of the matter was, Barbra was Jonathon's aunt. Family. Barbra would be there long after she had returned to her safe life. She had no right to deny Barbra, even if in her heart of hearts she didn't want her. Barbra's sins of omission had unsettled Liane, upsetting the balance of trust. Still, she knew better than to oppose her.

'That would be wonderful, Barbra,' Liane lied politely. 'I know Jonathon would want you there, and you will be company for me.'

'Splendid!' Barbra looked up at Julian, with a sparkle in her dark eyes. 'Liane and I will be able to handle anything together.'

Julian looked unimpressed. 'One of my people will go with you in any case.'

'What, do you mean a bodyguard?' Barbra asked.

'Staff. A man to ensure the household is secure.'

'Can you spare Barry Wiseman?' Barbra asked archly.

'Wiseman I had in mind.'

Barbra smiled and shot a playful glance at Liane. 'Such a lovely man, and devoted to Julian. Why, I swear he'd give his life for him. You two should have something in common, Liane. Barry paints for a hobby. He's surprisingly good, too. I think he could have made a go of it if he hadn't signed up with Wilde Holdings.' Her tone implied he was also very attractive and Liane would find him so.

'If you don't mind, Julian,' Liane said, 'I must go home.'

'I'll drive you,' he said decisively.

'I have my car here.'

'Shall I come with you?' Barbra suggested. 'I could help you organise a few things.'

'Please, I'd rather go alone. I'll be a lot faster that way.'

'As you wish,' Julian said shortly, inclining his imperious dark head. 'I'll get on to our real estate people. It has just occurred to me Nick de Lucca's place might be available. The compound is the last word in security. I've been there a few times with Nick and his wife. It would be perfect if Nick's not using it.'

'Be certain all you have to do is ask,' Barbra told him drily. 'You've done wonders for de Lucca's interests.'

'He's a good man.' Julian frowned. 'How long do you think you'll need, Liane?'

Liane had the sensation of rushing into even more threatening relationships. 'It all depends on Sir Eric.'

That had the effect of a red flag on a charging bull. 'You're saying Mossleigh comes first?' Julian towered over her, his face coldly brilliant.

'You'll be able to handle him, dear,' Barbra encouraged her. 'You're used to handling him, aren't you?'

Surely that wasn't craftiness in Barbra's dark eyes. Liane felt so pressurised she couldn't even begin to grapple with her mounting problems. 'Hopefully, I should be back here tonight. Certainly in time to see Jonathon before bed.'

'Great!' Barbra applauded. 'I can't hide my happiness this morning.'

Sir Eric, on the contrary, couldn't hide his anger. 'This is what I feared,' he told Liane in response to her request for time off. 'This will bring you back into Wilde's clutches.' He stared at her for a long moment, his handsome face taut and strained.

'It's Jonathon, Sir Eric.' Liane was upset by his reaction. 'No one wants to see a little boy suffer any trauma. I need to help him over it.'

'But the boy has family!' Sir Eric announced explosively. 'There's the aunt, that Edwards woman. Don't tell me she's not competent. A born manipulator if ever I saw one, and I'm an expert. There's Wilde himself, a houseful of staff, the boy's maternal grandparents. The Edwardses are extremely well placed.'

'I understand Jonathon doesn't see a lot of them. They've retired to Mount Tryon. You might not know.'

'All the better. The scenery is exquisite there.'

'Jonathon wants *me*.'

Sir Eric smoothed an agitated hand over the silver wing of his dark hair. 'Sometimes I could almost wish you weren't so lovable. Wilde is as deep and turbulent a man as I've ever known. All he has ever brought you is harm.'

And ecstasy. Beauty and brutality. 'There is nothing left between Julian and me,' Liane promised him. 'Apart from his little son. If you had seen Jonathon's face when he opened his eyes and recognised me...' Liane broke off as she saw Sir Eric was more exasperated than sympathetic.

'I thought all this business was finished.' He stopped in his pacing, looking at Liane intently. 'You don't really want to go, do you?'

'No.' Liane lifted her blue-green eyes.

'Because you don't want to come into close contact with Wilde.'

'No. I don't.' Liane bent her head for a moment. 'Pain lingers. You will know that.'

'He wants you back, of course.'

'He thinks of me as his possession, yes.'

'God, I could kill the man with my bare hands.' Sir Eric was acting so out of character Liane wished the whole meeting was over. She had only just begun to sense the deep feeling in him, now it was violently on show. A raging jealousy was in his face and voice.

'There is a solution, you know,' he said forcefully.

Under his intense scrutiny Liane felt her colour rise. 'I don't think so. I feel committed to helping Jonathon. This is a young life. I couldn't bear to allow a setback to alter his personality. I know I can help him cope with this experience very quickly.'

'Ah, yes,' Sir Eric replied grimly. 'But how are you going to cope yourself? When I offered you a job two years ago you were a desperately unhappy young woman. I've seen that change. Before this happened you were remarkable for your calm poise. You'd sorted out your pain and sense of loss. You let go. Now Wilde has swept back into your life and roused all those old anxieties. As well he might! I've said it before and I'll say it again. He's a dangerous man. Dangerous to you. I won't have it.'

'Please, Sir Eric,' Liane protested, almost gritting her white teeth. 'I had no idea you would take this so badly.'

'Had you not?' He suddenly swooped and lifted her to her feet. 'Answer me truthfully, Liane, and please stop calling me Sir Eric. How I hate it! You know I care deeply for you.'

'I'm sorry.' Her low, lovely voice was full of embarrassment and regret.

'Don't be sorry. Be glad. Look at me, Liane.' He shook her. 'I'm a powerful man. I can give you anything you want.'

'You shouldn't talk like this, Sir Eric, please.'

'It's about time, my girl, you got yourself remarried,' he told her bluntly. 'All this being on your own isn't good. I know you're highly intelligent, I never had a better secretary, but you're wasted in an office. You could turn your attention to charitable organisations. You could get out and meet people. Important people. As my wife!'

Liane was so shattered she felt like laughing hysterically. What was the basis for this love? Her face? Her body? Her efficiency and calm and poise? Feeling had to be mutual before a man could talk like this.

'Liane, my lovely girl,' Sir Eric said unsteadily, 'I do believe you're shocked.'

'I am,' she said finally, defeated by his tenderness. 'I'm so sorry, Sir Eric, I truly wasn't aware of your feelings.'

'But you are now?'

How could they ever turn back after this? She had even lost her job. 'I do like and respect you greatly.'

'And you believe that's nothing?' He tilted her chin.

'You're lonely, Sir Eric. Lonely since your wife died.'

'My dear.' He stroked her cheek lightly with his hand. 'I never loved a woman in my life until I met you. I never even knew what love was. From the moment I looked on your lovely face, my heart sang. I tried to make you see what your husband, your ex-husband, was like. I know I can't match him in terms of either youth or physical appeal, but I do know I could make you very happy.'

'Please, Sir Eric,' Liane said emotionally, 'you're making me sad.'

'That's because I've shocked you,' he told her indulgently. 'You need time. Time to be completely sure I can offer you the life you really want. Never in all the years of my marriage, and I was very fond of my wife, did I consider for a moment betraying her. Adultery destroys love. It sweeps the ground from beneath the feet of the betrayed one. I swear I'll dedicate the rest of my life to making you happy. I'm fifty-two and I keep myself very fit. We could have children. Our own son.'

'You have sons,' Liane answered quickly.

'Yes, yes.' Sir Eric nodded his head brusquely. 'But I don't consider they'll be ready to step into my shoes. To be frank, my sons are a disappointment to me. They're competent men, to be sure, but they show no sign of brilliance. Or aggression. A man like Wilde is their easy master in every respect. Even as an enemy I have to admit he's got flair. It's his thirst for women that's so shocking.'

Liane was stung by the magnitude of the charge. 'I can't help thinking that's largely a media creation,' she said angrily.

'Come, come, Liane. Wilde radiates a sexuality that's not quite decent.'

'Please, I don't want to speak any more about it.'

'Don't turn your head. Oh, God.' Sir Eric gripped her chin tighter. 'Let me kiss you.'

She began to pull away, agonised, but the energy suddenly ran out of her body. He lowered his head and claimed her lips, the pressure of his mouth increasing as the vigour of his feelings gripped him.

It was an extraordinary sensation. At first Liane could not believe this impeccably controlled man, this man she had hitherto seen only as a much respected employer, could be kissing her so eagerly, murmuring to her as he did so, his hands coming up, oh so reverently, to cup her face. He was trembling right through his body yet it was at once apparent he would not be an unsatisfactory lover. Sir Eric knew what he was about, and an odd spasm of response shook her. Powerful in the ways of the world, he had little use for hesitancy. He rained kisses on her face and her neck, obsessed by the thrill of touching her.

Shock immobilised her but only for a few moments. She broke away, stunned by this revelation, knowing her career in big business was over.

'My dear...Liane...' Sir Eric's handsome face was flushed with blood. 'Forgive me. I've come on so strongly, when all I wanted to do was kiss your sweet lips. Please say I haven't upset you.'

Liane found she couldn't answer. She didn't know it, but she had lost all her colour as she always did when she went into shock.

'If you only knew how I've wanted to take you in my arms,' he said in an impassioned voice. 'Advise and protect you. Don't you know you've always turned to me? These past two years have been wonderful, then again they've been a torment. I've been living for the day when you'd purge Wilde from your heart and mind. Now this. One could almost think it was a deliberate act.'

'No!' Liane looked up at those stern, distinguished features.

'I'd never be amazed at anything Wilde would do. If you knew as much about him as I do! The deals he has pulled off and in the most unorthodox ways. He's capable of doing anything to get what he wants.' Sir Eric's voice crackled with hate.

'You think he would put his own little son through an ordeal to get to me?' Liane asked, aghast.

'Even that.'

'That's madness, Sir Eric, and you know it.'

'All I know is, I love you, and now you're fully aware of it.'

Despite herself Liane felt touched. 'I'm sorry,' she murmured. 'So sorry, but I can never return your love.'

'Because you won't free yourself from this obsession with Wilde.'

'I have!' Liane threw back her golden head. 'I left him and I have *stayed* away.'

'I don't care.' Sir Eric's expression turned to iron. 'You've run to him now.'

'For *Jonathon*.'

Sir Eric refused to accept it. He came to her and placed his hands firmly on her shoulders. 'If you truly believe that, one of the best protections you could have is to tell Wilde you are soon to marry me.'

Liane gave an hysterical little laugh. 'That would be positively dangerous.'

'Do you think I wouldn't protect you?' A hard aggression crept into Sir Eric's cultured voice.

'How? You wouldn't be there.'

'I'm always here, my dear. It might come as a shock to you, but Wilde and I are deadly enemies. He's not ready yet to move against me. For all his brilliance, a wrong move could cost him. Rich as he is, he's still trailing behind me. I was used to getting what I wanted when he was only playing with toy cars.'

'This is unbelievable!' Liane said, trying desperately to regain some sense of balance. 'I feel like a pawn between you. Absurd, isn't it?'

Sir Eric lifted her slender hand, turned it over and kissed the palm. 'You are the first person in my life I've ever loved in this way. It doesn't take anything from my late wife. We had a good marriage. She brought me peace and order, two sons, but you take my breath away. It happened the first time I looked into your eyes. You probably don't remember. It was at a garden party for one of the Queen's visits. You were wearing a most beautiful dress and a large filmy hat. You hadn't been married very long, and Wilde was fiercely possessive of you. He would have avoided me if he could. To the rest of the world we're part of the same establishment. After all, his father was my deputy at one time. But we knew all the deals were only weapons. Wilde is out to destroy me.'

Out of nowhere Liane was suddenly conscious of the truth. It was as though a multitude of veils had fallen from her eyes. 'So,' she said bleakly, 'how was it this vendetta started? Was it something to do with his father?'

'Ask Wilde,' Sir Eric returned fiercely. 'He blames me for his father's terrible failure. For the fact that Jonathon Wilde took his own life.'

'What gave him that idea?' Liane challenged, looking directly into Sir Eric's grey eyes.

'Unquestionably he was looking for a scapegoat. He idolised his father. His father could do no wrong. Society disavows suicides.'

'Julian saw his father's death as a terrible accident. Suicide was never proved at the inquest.'

'It was suicide all right,' Sir Eric said. 'I didn't speak at the inquest, but I know.'

'You can't really know,' Liane said with the will to resist him.

'I wasn't the only one to see it as suicide. Wilde was ruined. All his super moves had gone wrong. It's a brave or foolish man who seeks to move against me.'

'So you were involved?' Liane had a crazy impulse to switch on the recorder.

Sir Eric's heavy lids came down to mask his eyes. 'Jonathon Wilde ruined himself. He did that without my lifting a finger. I have always regretted that he never came to me to try to straighten things out. I suspected what he was doing, of course. Once he was my partner, then he defected to the other side. He had no capacity for withstanding a huge reversal. I'm proud to say *I* have. Had Jonathon Wilde stayed with me, his son's life would have been different. He would have come into the organisation. Now he's thinking of crossing me, like his father he won't survive.'

'I know Julian,' Liane replied. 'He'll survive and endure. He doesn't live with illusions. He's strong.'

'So how come you're not together?' Sir Eric smiled unpleasantly.

'Perhaps someone wanted us apart.' Liane found her voice.

'No, my dear,' Sir Eric said in a quiet, pitying tone. 'Don't let your lingering feeling for him play you false. Wilde is a betrayer.'

Liane could barely bring herself to say another word. Betrayer. She was conscious of Lesley Bannigan's voice ringing in her ears.

*I'd renounce the world for Julian, but all he wants is an affair. Someone casual to bring him change. Men are all betrayers, darling. Grow up and accept it.*

Well, she had grown up but she still couldn't accept it.

'What are you going to do?' Sir Eric asked, watching the play of emotions across her lovely face.

Liane bent to pick up her soft leather handbag. 'My duty as I see it.' She turned to face him composedly. 'Jonathon grew from two to four with me. It was no ordinary relationship. Our love survived. He could have forgotten me. Many another child would, but like his father and his grandfather before him he has a long memory.'

'How long do you suppose it will take?' Sir Eric fastidiously readjusted the slip of maroon silk in his breast pocket.

'The problem is I don't know.'

'So you admit there is a problem?'

'Yes.' Her eyes were as brilliant as jewels. 'I thought I had put the past behind me, but I haven't. I don't understand why Julian has this power over me, but he has.'

'Then protect yourself!' Sir Eric exhorted her. 'My God, someone has to help you before you fall into his clutches again. He'll take you and use you as he did before. I can't bear that. You're beautiful and sweet and clever. You deserve the best. A man who will offer you his whole heart. His devotion. I've waited for you all this time, but I'm out of patience. I realise now that you weren't aware of my love. I wanted to give you time, but time is running out. I want you *now*. I need you desperately. I'm no ordinary man. I can give you everything your heart desires. You responded to me just now. You know you did. I can teach you how to love me. I can give you back your self-respect. Wilde will only degrade you.'

'Please, Sir Eric.'

'*Eric,*' he prompted her with a flash of extreme impatience.

'Eric,' she returned gravely. 'I don't love you. You honour me with your affections, but I have never thought of you in that way.'

'Are you worried about the age difference?' He looked up from beneath frowning brows.

'If I loved you it wouldn't make a difference. You're a very fit and handsome man.'

'Yes, I am!' Sir Eric agreed quite matter-of-factly. 'Believe me, I'm ready to father our child. A beautiful child. Could it be anything else?'

Liane was conscious of a feeling of sickness. 'I must go,' she said, facing him.

'Promise me you'll keep in contact,' he begged her urgently. 'You owe me that, Liane.'

'I do. No one has been kinder to me than you have.' It was nothing less than the truth. He had been kindness itself.

He stared at her for a long moment, drinking in her youth and beauty. 'I've shocked you today, my darling girl, but I know from long experience how quickly new ideas sink in. Tomorrow you'll begin thinking of me as your suitor, not your employer. You've changed my world, Liane. Now let me change yours.'

# CHAPTER FOUR

CASAMIA, the De Lucca beach home, was poised on a private peninsula overlooking the deep blue waters of the Pacific. De Lucca, a construction giant, had poured millions of dollars into his magnificent property, secluded in its prime position from the rest of the beach community, but only a short distance by car from a major resort with all its shops and restaurants and entertainments.

'Isn't this marvellous, Dad!' Jonathon cried. It was good to see him so bright and interested when he had suffered nightmares during the night. 'I don't like it as much as Sandpiper, but it's still nice.'

Nice was scarcely the word. It was a masterpiece of contemporary design, a beach paradise set in five lush palm-studded acres and completely surrounded by a fortress-like wall, affording complete privacy and, along with a monitoring system, total security. Outbuildings included a guest cottage, a staff cottage and screened bushhouses for orchids and house plants maintained by the full-time gardener. De Lucca himself rarely saw it these days, he was so committed to business expansion, but he was delighted to make it available to a good friend.

'There are lots of great places to play!' Jonathon exclaimed excitedly as they swept up the royal-palm-lined drive. 'I love the beach best of all. I can't wait to go for a swim. How long are you going to stay, Daddy?'

'Until tomorrow.' Julian smiled and squeezed his son's hand, resting over on his shoulder. 'I promise I'll get up here every weekend.'

74

'Did you hear that, Lee?' Jonathon cried excitedly, peering around to see Liane's face. 'Now you and Dad will be together again.'

'I'm sure Liane realises that.' Julian glanced sideways at Liane's pure profile, sapphire eyes glinting. 'Sit down now, Jonathon. You should never stand up in cars.'

'But we're nearly there, Dad. I don't need my seat-belt any more.'

'And what if a dog should suddenly run across the drive and I'd have to brake?'

'I'd fall backwards, I guess.' Jonathon collapsed on to the seat cheerfully. 'I'm so happy I feel as if everything is shining like Lee's hair.'

Permanent staff looked after the house, a husband-and-wife team, and now they came out to greet the visitors and take care of the luggage.

The wife was a charming, motherly-looking woman, and Liane took to her at once, while the husband looked equally kind and competent, with a brown, liquid gaze. They were Italian migrants, in the country less than five years, but their English was good.

The wife, who asked to be called Rosa, showed them over the house before going away to prepare a lunch she promised would be served *al fresco* on the terrace.

Jonathon ran excitedly from room to room admiring everything as he went. 'I've got to get into my togs!'

'Not until after lunch, Jonathon.' Liane steadied him. 'Why don't you put your things away in the wardrobe?'

'Will you help me?'

'In a little while. I have to talk to Daddy.'

'Oh, sure.' Jonathon smiled delightedly. 'You still love him, right?'

'Out of the mouths of babes,' Julian jeered sardonically.

'I'm afraid, Julian,' Liane said suddenly, 'Jonathon thinks you and I have come together again.'

'Damn right we have!'

Liane swirled to face him, her hair in the sunlight making a bright halo around her face. 'For a few weeks, Julian, I told you.'

'Are you ready to leave as soon as you've arrived?' he asked sarcastically.

'You *know* what I mean. It would be cruel to allow Jonathon to think I'm going to stay.'

'How much would it take?' Julian asked her.

Her eyes darkened to jade. 'You can't be talking money?'

He shrugged. The sea breeze tousled his hair so that it broke into crisp curls and waves. 'How does ten million sound to you?'

'Ridiculous.'

'You want more?'

'I don't want your money at all,' she said disdainfully.

'I guess good old Eric has promised you more.'

'He *has!*' Stung, she burst into speech when she should have remained silent.

Julian's sardonic smile disappeared in an instant. 'You mean the old fool has asked you to marry him?' he demanded harshly.

Liane turned to grip the balustrade, looking out over the dazzling blue ocean. 'I don't have to discuss my private affairs with you.'

'So he did.'

'I told you, Julian, to leave me alone.' Her voice shook.

'I'll never let that happen, Liane.' He came to stand beside her, looking down at her with a purpose that frightened her. 'I would not dare to speak of it again if I were you. Mossleigh will *not* have anything that is *mine.*'

'Isn't there something you're forgetting? You don't *own* me. Women have escaped from their bonds.'

'None of us escape our *emotional* bonds,' Julian pointed out tensely. 'That's where the danger lies. Feeling in its extreme forms makes us break away from the restrictions society imposes on us. As it happens, you are my wife. Our marriage, to me, wasn't a temporary thing, some game I engaged in. It was the most profound act of my life. In order for our divorce to work I have to accept it, and I don't. You have no independence from me. Whichever way you turn, I'll cut you off.'

'You need help.' Liane charged him emotionally. 'Your obsessions are taking you further and further away from reality.'

'If that's true for me it's true for you. You could not have had a more loving husband, yet on the basis of an ugly lie you turned away from me in hate. I never expected to be so dishonoured by my own wife.'

'You assume I would accept your larger desires?'

Julian threw back his raven head and gazed balefully at the sky. 'Must I stress again that your *stupidity* pushed you into divorce? Your own lack of security? I've had to see it as the result of a deprived childhood. I know your grandmother was a wonderful woman—would that she had been alive to talk some sense to you—but you grew up without parents. You lost the two people in the world most important to your development. I think you were traumatised.'

'You would!' She was seized by anger and her own remembered anguish. 'You're insufferable, Julian. I hate you. I must be mad to come anywhere near you.' Frantically she backed away, but as she did so she came to the end of the deck. It was a total surprise and she seemed to arch backwards, strangely disorientated.

'For God's sake!' Underneath his copper tan Julian's face was white. 'What are you trying to do?' His arms were around her powerfully, seizing her to him. 'There's a twenty-foot drop there.'

She could have cried aloud with her need, the sheer throb of desire. Her body had been starved of his for two years. An eternity. He had taught her all there was to know about passion, about tenderness and ardour, and she had been forced to live in celibacy.

'Liane.' He tipped back her head, her long hair falling down her back, looking into her strangely wild eyes. *'Liane!'* He pressed her harder against his body, so that she could feel his arousal, but her eyes flashed anger and the fierce resistance of the unbearably tempted. 'Tell me you don't want me.' She stared back at him wordlessly, the two of them locked in a violent embrace. 'Come on, convince me.'

'You just want to own me.'

He laughed, a bitter little laugh without humour. 'Whatever. I never fail to arouse you.'

'Why not?' It was futile to struggle. 'You set your mind to it.'

'Mind?' His blue eyes flashed down at her. 'It's my body that's half crazy. You're just the same. We're both being tortured.'

Goaded, she thudded her fist against his chest but he only crushed her to him, and as his anger soared he took her mouth, cutting off her frantic little protestations. She was drained of all hope, all resistance, all everything. Their teeth and tongues clashed. It wasn't love but a kind of violence. She could have killed him for his control of her, yet her body responded like a wild thing, deeply addicted to his touch.

'Yes, oh yes...' he muttered against her open mouth. 'You've never learned to want anyone else.'

'And what are you?' she cried furiously, golden spangles in her iridescent eyes. 'The way you treat me. What are you? Some sort of a pirate?'

'Let me love you,' he muttered violently. 'All over again.'

'No.' She tried to turn her head aside. 'You should have horns growing out of your head.'

'Oh, well.' A laugh shook him.

'I don't want to know.'

'You *do* know. What am I supposed to do, go down on my knees? Beg your forgiveness? For what? Your bloody stupidity?'

'Don't start.' She was beside herself with shame. She wanted him to ravish her.

'Dad, Lee?' Jonathon spoke from somewhere behind them with an ease that amazed her. Julian spun around, his beautiful, rare smile lighting his face. 'How's it going?'

'Great!' Jonathon's blue eyes sparkled with mischief. 'I saw you kissing Lee.'

'Clap away,' Julian told him.

Jonathon did, his small face aglow with happiness. 'You must have missed us, Lee, like we missed you.'

'Sure did, darling.' Only now could Liane break away from Julian. She looked beguilingly lovely, with hectic colour in her cheeks and her eyes sparkling like the sun on the sea.

'I was afraid I'd never see you again,' Jonathon confessed, 'but Dad always told me we would. He said you had to be on your own for a little while before you came home.'

'Your father has great skill at determining people's lives.'

'Dad's really clever,' Jonathon agreed, not understanding. 'I wish Aunty Barbra wasn't coming.'

'Darling, she loves you.' Liane was faintly shocked.

'She gives me toys.' Jonathon tried to recall something. 'Wait until you see my Defender game. It's electronic.'

'And Barbra gave you that?' Liane's hand clenched.

'Yes, she did, for my birthday. Want me to go and get it?'

'If you don't mind.'

'I've got games two people can play,' Jonathon told her happily. 'We're going to have a great time.'

'What's the matter, Liane?' Julian asked her, after Jonathon had gone.

'I'm sure I bought a game called Defender. Perhaps I'm wrong. It was certainly electronic.'

'And this was for Jonathon's birthday?'

'Yes, it was. Probably Barbra bought something similar. They're all the rage for kids.'

'Odd the things our fellow human beings get up to.'

'So you do believe I bought the presents?' She glanced into his glinting eyes.

'Unlike you, I'm not subject to doubts about people I'm supposed to love,' he told her acidly.

Jonathon ran back, holding a video game in his hand. 'Here it is, Lee. I have to say Aunty Barbra gives me great presents. But she never plays with me.'

'Is that it?' Julian asked.

'It's exactly similar. That's all I can say.' Liane stooped to look at it. Jonathon was looking at her, waiting for a response of some kind. 'It looks fun,' she smiled.

'And you can play with it,' Jonathon promised. 'When is lunch going to be ready? I'm hungry.'

'Let's go and see.' Liane ruffled his curls. 'Isn't this a beautiful place?'

'Beautiful!' Jonathon exclaimed, slipping his arm around Liane's waist and waiting for his father to catch up with them. 'The sun is so hot it's going to be marvellous in the water. I hope you brought your swim suit, Lee.'

'Not only that, I've brought two and they're new. It's a long time since I've had a beach holiday.'

'Christmas three years ago,' Julian confirmed briefly. 'For someone so fair you go golden in the sun.'

Lunch was served on the terrace, under a big yellow umbrella thickly fringed in white. Around them were the sounds of the surf and seagulls diving on the waves in search of fish. Terracotta urns spilled flowers, geraniums, impatiens, white petunias and sun jewels, and the air smelled of pines and salt. It was beautiful, blue and golden, and they were united in a deep appreciation of their glorious surroundings. Mrs Morona provided them with a superb selection: succulent scallops served on a bed of saffron rice with lemon and parsley, followed by camembert chicken, new potatoes and green salad with avocado dressing. Jonathon even had the space for mango ice-cream, but Julian and Liane finished the delicious meal with a cheese platter and a glass of very good red wine.

'What about a little nap?' Liane suggested. 'No more than an hour. You had a disturbed night.'

'Do I have to, Lee?'

'Yes, you do,' his father said firmly. 'I have a few calls to make and afterwards we'll all go for a swim.'

In his room, Jonathon pulled Liane's head down and kissed her. 'I used to pretend you were always with me. When the kids asked where my mother was, I always said "at home."'

'Did you, darling?' Liane studied his earnest face.

'Don't ever go away again, will you?'

'Let's say I don't want to ever leave you.'

'Don't you love Dad?'

'Sometimes grown-up people have problems, Jonathon.'

'It looked like you loved him when you were kissing him.'

'Your father is the best kisser in the world!'

'Stop!' Jonathon giggled. 'Is he really?'

'You'd better believe it! Now turn over and have forty winks. I'll get settled in my room.'

Mrs Morona had allotted her the master bedroom under instructions from Nick de Lucca. Husband and wife had been told to leave no stone unturned to ensure his guests had 'the holiday of a lifetime'.

Liane walked out on to the private deck, looking down at the magnificent beach front. De Lucca had planted some three hundred palm trees, so the grounds resembled a marvellous tropical plantation. Beyond the brilliant blue length of the swimming pool with its swirling mosaic design on the bottom was the ocean in all its glory, and Liane started to remember all the beach picnics they had had at Sandpiper. Never in a hundred lifetimes could she lock her memories away. And what of Jonathon? Was it wise to allow him to believe she and Julian had come together again? Julian had given her the greatest happiness and unhappiness she had ever known.

With a sigh she turned away and walked back into the magnificent master bedroom. It was furnished in white and sand colours with touches of brilliant blue and Thai green. Hibiscus and bird of paradise were used for the floral decorations and the whole ambience was of relaxation and romance. Liane remembered that Nick De Lucca had a very beautiful wife.

She selected her swimsuit and went into the bathroom to put it on. She was lily white. In the days of her marriage she had always had a summer tan. Julian had been mad for water sports since childhood and he excelled at all of them. She wondered what had happened to the yacht *Lady Elizabeth*, named for his mother. It had its private marina at Sandpiper.

The streamlined one-piece, aqua in colour, looked nothing off but sensational on the body. She felt too conscious of Julian's eyes on her to risk the brief bikini. She would wear that when he had gone back to the city. She drew her long hair into a topknot, coiled it, and pinned it to her head. Like Julian and Jonathon, she delighted in the water, and she was looking forward to diving under the crystal purity of those full, rolling waves.

Her spirits were soaring despite the disturbing stimulus of Julian's presence. For the first time in a long time she felt a great uprush of hope. Feelings just wouldn't let a person be, feelings so powerful they even dominated Julian. Was it possible she had come to mean more to him after the divorce? It seemed his next major step was to buy her back, but never again on his terms. There was no compromise solution. Much as she loved Jonathon she wasn't going to be blackmailed. Whatever she learned in life it would not be to accept infidelity. She could not be alternately loved and abandoned. The grief was too much.

Jonathon slept peacefully for forty-five minutes and woke up refreshed. Liane remained close by, keeping an eye on him. She had seen the fright in his face when she had had to shake him out of a nightmare the night before. There was no evidence of that in the brilliant light of day.

Julian was still on the phone when they made their way down to the beach. He waved to them as they passed and Jonathon gave his father an eager, 'Hurry up!'

'Sometimes I wish Dad didn't have so much work,' he told Liane. 'He's never off the phone. He even has them in the cars.'

Nevertheless Julian did make it down to the beach, wearing black swimming-briefs with a cobalt blue and black striped beach towel over his shoulder. His lean, athletic body was deeply tanned, marvellous to look upon. He really was a spell-binding man, Liane thought wryly. Couldn't she have fallen in love with a normal, likable guy? It was an effort to withdraw her eyes from his lean, superbly conditioned physique.

'Let's have a bet here,' he said briskly to Jonathon. 'Last in has to cut dinner and we're going out!'

'Get up, Lee,' Jonathon urged, 'this is important!'

Liane really tried, but she couldn't beat them into the water.

'No matter, Lee,' Jonathon consoled her, 'Dad would never leave you at home. Don't take it seriously.'

The water was perfection, tingling at first, then gloriously cool. It was like going back in time to those halcyon days when the three of them were perfectly integrated. Julian and Jonathon stayed in when Liane went out to sunbathe, and she lay back on her towel with the warm sunshine gilding her body and limbs. The time she spent in the water was enough for her face. She knew she looked good with a light tan. It did marvellous things for her hair and eyes. Her fears were receding under the healing power of sun and surf, so when Julian came out of the water leaving Jonathon playing a game on the edge, she opened her eyes to smile at him.

'That was marvellous!'

'So's your smile!' His blue eyes moved over her, a devastating twist to his mouth. 'Your skin is like milk.'

'I know. It will only take a day or two to change all that.'

'What about our lives?'

'Just let me be, Julian.'

'Darling,' he said lightly, 'you're in for worse shocks.'

'What does that mean?' She sat up.

'Maybe I'll tell you later.' He towelled himself off then lay down beside her. 'I rather like you in that aqua thing, but whatever happened to the little bits of nothing you used to wear?'

'Curiously, you make me terribly self-conscious.'

'You never were before.'

'Don't tease.' Her heart pounded. 'I can't take it.'

'Want some oil?'

'No, thank you.'

'Surely a little on your back?'

'What are you trying to do to me, Julian?'

'Nothing. Jonathon will be here in a minute. Well, what about some oil?'

'You know as well as I do, your touch seems to trigger things off.'

'And there's not much we can do about it.'

'Ever heard of self-discipline?'

'I sleep on my own every night.'

'You can do what you want. It's not my affair any more.'

'You never were any good at pretending.'

They stayed on the beach for most of the afternoon, sunbathing, playing ball, diving into the waves to cool off, finally going for a long walk while Jonathon scouted up shells. It was one of the most simple and positive forms of pleasure, and as Julian took Liane's arm to help her back up the stairs to the house, she didn't pull away, but clung to him as once she had done.

It had been decided that in Julian's absence they would dine at home at night, but on this occasion he drove them into the resort where he had booked dinner at an excellent though slightly out of the way restaurant. The locals knew it as offering the best food in town, but the tourists and the trendies usually frequented the more visible nightspots.

Jonathon was so excited they were all together he could barely eat. He sat in his chair staring from one to the other, conveying a picture of innocence and trust. *You are my world*, he seemed to be saying, and more than once Liane found her eyes misting over. A child had such need of love and protection. She caught his small hand and pressed it and he smiled back at her with unquestioning acceptance. There was no doubt Liane was a very important person in his young life.

Across the table from her, Julian looked stunningly handsome in a royal blue linen sports jacket over a white collarless shirt and linen slacks. A few hours in the sun and his tan had intensified, making his eyes blaze like sapphires in a bronze sculpture.

'I haven't relaxed like this in a long while.'

'So what do you want to go away for, Dad?' Jonathon asked. 'We had such a great time this afternoon.'

'I'll come back as soon as I can. Inevitably, business calls. Wilde Holdings are expanding rapidly. I plan to outlay many millions for a thirty-per cent interest in a UK Industrial Group. That's off the record, Liane, just in case you're planning to relay it to your ex-boss.'

Jonathon's flower-blue eyes widened. 'Aren't you working for Sir Eric Mossleigh any more, Lee?'

She gazed back at him for a long moment, her changeable eyes darkened to the leaf-green of her silk dress. Her long, pale golden hair swirled around her face like the hair of an angel in a Botticelli painting, and her expression was grave. 'I'm not exactly sure of my plans, Jonathon.'

'Don't go back to him, Lee,' Jonathon begged. 'Dad doesn't like it.'

'We all need money to survive, darling. I have to work for a living.'

Very deliberately Julian drained his wine-glass. 'Working was your choice.'

'Dad has tons of money, Lee,' Jonathon told her earnestly. 'Why won't you let him give you some?'

'When you're older, darling, you'll understand about independence. Each of us must make a meaningful life for ourselves. We cannot depend totally on anyone else.'

'I suppose not.' Jonathon nodded his head wisely. 'Aunty Barbra said she was delighted you were so noble.'

'Roll that past me again, Jonathon,' Julian said. 'Were those her exact words, or only what you recall?'

'You know Mrs Parrish? She was speaking to her. She said, "I'm delighted the dear girl is so noble." They were talking about you, Lee. It may have been wrong, but I hung around to hear.'

'And Barbra is arriving tomorrow?' Julian started to laugh. A faintly menacing sound. 'I have to agree nobility is the word.'

Liane took sugar from a silver bowl and stirred a little into her black coffee. 'Perhaps she meant nothing. She told me many times I should have accepted a settlement.'

'Let's toss her out,' Jonathon suddenly exclaimed, sounding so much like his father that even Liane was startled.

'That's not very nice, darling.'

'And it wouldn't be easy either.'

'That's enough, Jonathon,' Julian said firmly. 'Since Barbra is your aunt and Liane's friend, we show her courtesy. There is a point, however...'

'Please, Julian,' Liane said quickly. 'Jonathon is nearly falling asleep at the table. All that sun and surf. I think we should take him home.'

Thirty-five minutes later, Liane turned down Jonathon's bed and waited for him to hop in.

'That's rotten toothpaste,' he said.

'I'll get the brand you're used to in the morning. At least you no longer eat it.'

'I hope I'm not going to have any more nightmares.' He watched her gliding around him, putting his clothes away.

'You sound to me as if you enjoy having a little company during the night.'

'Will you come, Lee?'

'Of course I will, darling.' She bent down to kiss him. 'But I know you're going to be perfectly all right. Your world is a safe place. Daddy is here and so am I.'

'I wouldn't want to make my Dad mad,' Jonathon said, in a ludicrously dry and adult tone. 'He's the best dad in the whole world. He's not afraid of anything. I've never been so happy in a long, long time. Don't work for Sir Eric Mossleigh any more. It makes Dad angry. He said he'll regret it.'

Liane looked down into his eyes. 'Who will?'

'Why, Sir Eric, of course. Dad usually watches it around me but he calls Sir Eric rude names. *Son of a bitch!*'

'Well, we won't say it again,' Liane said quickly. 'It's not terribly nice, and out of the question for a six-year-old boy.'

'If you think that's bad, you should hear the kids at school. My teacher says the whole world has gone mad.'

'There are a lot of good people in it. Always remember that, Jonathon.' Liane stroked his silky black curls back from his temples. 'Say a little prayer to your guardian angel and he will watch over you during the night.'

'Nobody talks to me about guardian angels any more. No one except you. I don't think my guardian angel is a he at all. I think of him as you.'

Liane switched off the light with a troubled heart. All she was doing was making things harder for Jonathon. He was making her too much the focus of his love.

When she returned downstairs Julian was making another of his high-level phone calls. She didn't particularly listen but at one point she heard him mention Altmann Industries and a Leo Dimock, chairman of the board. After that, she got up and walked outside on to the terrace.

The midnight-blue sky was crowded with stars, so big and brilliant they were like jewelled flowers thrown down on grape velvet. The air was so fresh and sweet and clean that she took long, deep, steadying breaths into her lungs. Her feelings of agitation began to intensify with the night. Mrs Morona had waited for them to return, and, satisfied they had everything they wanted, had retired to her bungalow near by.

Liane and Julian were on their own. Obviously Barbra hadn't thought of that, otherwise she would have made every effort to join them the first day. Why did Liane consider that now? Julian's security man wasn't arriving until the following day either, and Liane could only conclude Julian had arranged it that way. She tried to push away unsettling thoughts of Barbra. Jonathon was such a perceptive little boy. His teachers reported that he was highly intelligent, with a quick understanding far beyond his schoolmates, and those were the sons of the so-called élite. Jonathon did not like Barbra, and Liane was one of those people who recognised the intuitive responses of children. In Barbra's conversation with Maggie Parrish Jonathon had discerned a maliciousness in her, which in her dealings with Liane she always kept below the surface. Liane couldn't bear to look at the implications in more detail. She had gone all this time thinking of Barbra as her friend.

'There you are!' Julian came up behind her, his magnetism making her feel excited and tense. 'Jonathon asleep?'

'Almost as soon as his head touched the pillow.' She spoke into the dark, fragrant night. 'I don't think we'll have the panic of last night.'

'I hope to God not. I'm very proud of my son. He has coped with a great deal in his short life. In one way I'm able to give him everything, but he has never experienced the greatest gift of all: family love. He would

have had it from my mother and father. The Wildes
always knew how to show their love. His maternal
grandparents are something else again. I expect they
would have shown more interest in Jonathon had their
daughter lived or had he resembled their side of the
family more closely. As it is, he's all Wilde. You know
he'll refuse to let you go away.'

'That's cruel, Julian. Little as I want to believe it, I
think I'm only adding to Jonathon's problems. Did you
know he thinks of me as his guardian angel? Of course
I taught him that prayer when he was very tiny.'

'So what do you want to be?' Julian asked her in a
hard tone.

'Perhaps a close friend, if you will allow it.'

'He wants much more than that.'

'Then why don't you stop fooling around and give
him a mother?'

Despite herself Liane flared into sudden passion.
'Some compassionate young woman who will fill his
world with love and security. God knows there must be
plenty of them around.'

'There are plenty of phonies,' he told her harshly.
'Women are highly attracted to rich, available males.
Not a lot of them want to take on a child. Other women's
children drive them to despair. They only want to enjoy
their own. Almost no one is like you, Liane. If you
weren't so passionate you would have made a marvellous little nun, ministering to sick and sad humanity.'

'Don't spoil the night,' she said shakily. 'Barbra will
be here tomorrow.'

'So what about Barbra now?' Julian leaned against
the balustrade, staring at her averted profile. The breeze
off the ocean was lifting her long hair away from her
face like a gold banner. 'I've always had a strong suspicion of Barbra. A sort of bad feeling. Nothing I can
exactly define. More an intuition, like Jonathon's. I

always appreciated the way she was so very pleasant to you. She could have shown an unpleasant jealousy, after all. You replaced her sister, and she couldn't have been more helpful or supportive. It placed me in an awkward position. My feelings for her were always at war.'

'I understood you were attracted to both sisters,' said Liane.

'Have you lost all your marbles?'

'You deny it?'

'Why don't you turn and look at me?' he taunted her harshly.

'All right!' She swung around, her full skirt whipping around her slender legs. 'Eric told me.'

'Eric?'

'Don't yell at me,' she burst out.

'Amazing!' Julian's furious blue eyes roamed all over her face. 'Now she calls him Eric. Isn't that too, too precious!'

'Because he wants me to!'

'And what else does he want you to do?'

'Julian,' she said wretchedly. 'If you shout so much the Moronas will hear you.'

'Come back into the house. It's a big house. You don't have to get out on to the veranda for protection.'

'Where are we going?'

A muscle worked along his strong jaw. 'To the living-room, you little fool. Whatever you think of me, you must know I'd hesitate to rape my own wife.'

'Your ex-wife, for God's sake!'

'And you the one with strong moral values. *I* don't approve of divorce.'

'That's true. You think you're entitled to a wife and a mistress. Mistresses, for that matter. I detest men!'

'Now who's setting up the clamour?' He reached for her, pressing a hand against her mouth. 'Are you going to settle down?'

For answer, she bit his hand.

'I see,' he said simply. 'You want an outlet for your frustrations.' Something wild and taut sprang into his handsome face.

'I'm at your mercy, Julian. You arranged it like that.'

'You came!' His eyes flared at her.

'Can you live with what you're doing to me?' Tears sprang into her eyes, upsetting him so violently that he strained her to him.

'Don't, Liane.'

'We're pulling each other apart, can't you see that?'

'All I know is, I will want you all my life.'

'But you don't realise I can't live your life!' When he was holding her she was all soft despair. 'I love you too much, Julian!'

'You said it.' His eyes blazed.

'I *loved* you too much, Julian.' She looked up at him with fearful eyes. 'You know perfectly well what I mean.'

'I swear to you I will never look at another woman,' he promised fiercely. 'I certainly haven't, but you've got that firmly planted inside your head. Come back to me, Liane.'

'I won't be treated like some company! You're using the tactics of the boardroom.'

'It's better than beating you.' His voice took on a ruthless edge. 'You're terrified of my kissing you.'

She threw him a look of wild reproach. 'What's between us is finished, but you won't let go.'

'What's between us is love, Liane. Nothing will kill it.'

His expression was her undoing. 'Don't, Julian.' Tears filled her eyes, making them indescribably beautiful.

'Don't?' He gave an exclamation of impotent rage and lifted her off her feet, carrying her through to the living-room and sinking down on one of the deeply upholstered banquettes that formed a large semicircle along one wall. 'Have you been happy without me?' He demanded.

'At least I've had my self-respect.' She pushed back her tumbled hair.

'Working for Mossleigh?' he snapped.

'He was one of the few people who were kind to me. Everyone else seemed to side with you.'

'And you didn't think that was odd?'

'You've always had tons of charisma, and men always stick together. They don't find anything terribly ugly about adultery.'

'Let's leave adultery aside.' His chiselled face tightened, accentuating the lines that ran from nostril to lip.

'Suit yourself,' she laughed shakily. 'You always do. Why am I sitting in your lap?'

'Because you want to, I imagine.'

'Let me up!' She made as if to spring, but he pressed her back.

She saw his eyes were dangerous and she snapped her small white teeth. 'Possessions! That's all women are!'

'Then you should have no doubt you're mine.'

'I don't *want* to be. I can only say what is deepest in my heart.'

'Because you think I betrayed you once?'

'Are you trying to tell me there haven't been other women since we've been apart?'

'No, I'm not trying to tell you that.' He held her tighter as she rocked her body away from him. 'I'm not a monk. Neither am I in any way promiscuous. I am frequently asked to pose with women for photographs, but no one who really knows me could call me a womaniser. Rather the reverse. I don't go in for fun and games. I haven't the time or the inclination.'

'What am *I* then? Some kind of obsession?' She pressed her hands against his hard muscled chest. 'It's much too much for you to be a loser!'

Without warning his mood changed. His dark face poised over her became hard and alert, like a panther about to spring. He palmed over her breast, a gesture of possession that both angered and excited her. The tender-budded nipple tightened into arousal, straining against the silk. His fingers played with it, awakening all her senses, and she arched her back in response and denial.

'You're so beautiful!' he growled, lifting her closer into his arms and searching for her mouth.

'Oh, my God!' she breathed. 'Oh, my God!' Sensation was knifing through her and she flung out a hand as his mouth came down powerfully over hers, almost draining her breath. His hands controlled her writhing body. Nothing in the world was more shocking or more darkly desirable. Her nerves were jangling in her body, warming her and egging her on. She was so agitated she made little incoherent sounds every time his mouth freed her to find her neck or her ears or the hollow in her throat. Her physical need of him was an anguish even as she turned her head from side to side to ward him off.

Finally he clamped a hand to her cheeks so that there was nothing she could do but accept his devouring mouth. Then her golden head lay quite still, thrown back against his shoulder, but her body was shaking violently.

'Let me love you,' he muttered urgently, his blue eyes glittering. 'Now, Liane, the way I used to.'

Everything was whirling, not the effect of wine but that of too much excitement. He slid his hand beneath the crossover bodice of her dress, slipping the light lacy bra from her shoulder and claiming her naked breast. 'Little one! Your breasts are so delicate. So perfect!'

Her whole body shuddered in arousal and he bent his raven head, his mouth closing over the expectant rosebud, teeth gently nipping, then giving way to the claim of his hungry mouth.

'Julian!' she moaned as desire took over. Her frantic hands found his hair, her fingers sinking into his thick black curls. Her eyes were flickering beneath her fallen lids. He was driving her wild! 'I'm going to take you upstairs,' he told her tautly. 'I'm going to make love to you so that it will be impossible for you to leave me.'

They were in his room and he was peeling the clothes from her body.

'Two years!' He ran his hand triumphantly down her satiny nakedness, making her frantic for release. 'Do you know the anguish you caused me? *Two years* without my own wife!'

She rolled away with a low moan, burying her burning face in the cool nest of pillows. Hadn't she put herself in this forbidden position, risking everything? She was not prepared for a sexual encounter. She had lived in total chastity, faithful to her own code. Now she was consumed by a sudden terrible need, a need so overwhelming she was lying naked in Julian's bed, betrayed by her own sensuality. Why could she never, never withstand him? He had only to touch her and she went quickly from arousal to a desperate need for union with his heart-rending male body.

He came down beside her, his lean powerful frame freed from its clothes. He strained towards her. 'Come. Come here to me,' he said commandingly, palming her sloping shoulder and turning her into him. His eyes were so brilliant they had taken on the intensity of the possessed. '*Why* did you let us suffer?'

She was beyond answering, in the grip of his inexorable power.

'Liane!' With a low moan he lowered his head to her body so that, as though programmed, it flowered for his unending delight. His hands closed around her narrow waist, gripping as the pressure of his lips on her taut stomach made her sink into the bed. She stretched her legs, tantalised, passion rushing over her like a tidal wave. It had always been so! Such intimacies she allowed him she could never imagine with anyone else. He was so perfect to her. The force in him took her over the edge of control.

'Gently, darling.' He had to slow her. 'I want to make up for all the time we've missed.'

She didn't think she would be able to withstand the ecstasy. Her body was too responsive, tuned to a quivering pitch. Her teeth clenched and her nails bit into her palms.

'Julian!'

'Who else would it be?' he challenged her. 'No other man will ever have you!' She gasped as he deeply explored the most sensitive areas of her body. 'You're everything in the world I want.'

'And I want you!' She suddenly beat at him with her hands. *'Please.'*

He laughed exultantly. 'My girl. You're *my* girl!'

'I can't be.'

'And why not?' The strength of his hands hurt her. 'You can't have it every way you want. Only when I make love to you!'

'I don't care!' Her voice was as urgent as the blood roaring from her veins. Another moment and she would black out. 'Julian, I want you. Now!'

He threw his head back like a conqueror. 'I'll remind you of that in the sober light of morning. The time when you look as chaste as an angel.'

His powerful body shuddered. She could feel his violent ecstasy. It was her own.

Fulfilment was a tremendous thing. They came together in harmonious rhythmic motions, deeply unique and deeply private by design. Their bodies had been and continued to be marvellously attuned to each other. Liane cried out as the level of pleasure became almost intolerable, building to a climax annihilating in its power. Whatever conflicts had been played out, their bodies accepted their indestructible attraction.

Afterwards he continued to hold her in his arms, rocking her gently, murmuring into her damp hair.

Julian would always get what he wanted. No matter what the obstacles.

# CHAPTER FIVE

IN THE morning they were very quiet and careful with each other, as though words could shatter their fragile reconciliation. Jonathon slept right through the night but Liane did not return to her own bed until after Julian had awakened her with the dawn, reaching out and stroking her long hair away from her face, turning her very gently, meeting her soft, sleepy gaze. All that had changed. He had swept her into a sensual fantasy that even now, hours afterwards, made her skin glow incandescent as her blood continued to smoulder. Julian was the most sensuous and imaginative lover a woman could ever dream of, yet after the loving was over he was as cool as a cucumber, living only to become a financial giant.

'I'll keep in touch by phone,' he told them, 'and try to drive up Friday night. Barry should be here soon. I won't leave until he arrives.'

As it happened, Barbra arrived first in her white Alpine BMW 635. They all greeted her pleasantly, but for once Liane did not enjoy the older woman's effusive kiss. Was there a gloating behind the open demonstration of friendship? Now, for the first time, Liane was unsure.

'This is certainly satisfactory,' Barbra exclaimed when she was shown her luxurious room. 'To think de Lucca was a nothing and a no one! He should be grateful for what he has accomplished. I suppose one should applaud success.'

'Well, we're certainly grateful to him,' Liane answered.

'How's it going with Julian?' Barbra turned with great self-possession to give Liane a close stare. 'No bitter recriminations, I hope?'

Liane felt a catch high up under her heart. 'I'm older now. I'm beginning to listen.'

'To what?' Barbra lifted her arching brows. 'My dear, I'd be terribly shocked to hear Julian was weaving the old spells again. I know he's sexy enough to turn the strongest woman's head. It's only afterwards comes the torture.'

Liane shrugged. 'Being away from him is a torture of another kind. Anyway, let's drop this. I'm sure you'd like coffee.'

'Love one,' Barbra agreed, suddenly gnawing on her long, narrow top lip. 'Of course, you two were alone in the house last night. You had to be. I understood the security man would be here.'

'We're expecting him any minute.' Liane turned away from those dark, piercing eyes. 'It's going to be another glorious day. You've brought your swimsuit, I hope.' Actually she didn't care if Barbra swam or not.

'Of course I have, my dear. I'm not saying I'll go in. I hate getting covered in sand when I'm wet, but I intend to get a tan. A tan always suits me. I'd advise you to keep your white skin out of the sun, though.'

'You must have forgotten I'm one of those lucky blondes who tan beautifully,' Liane returned agreeably. 'Ah, here's Jonathon!' With a sense of relief she turned her head as Jonathon ran into the room.

'Steady, dear,' Barbra reproved him. 'One should never run in the house.'

'Sorry!' Jonathon's happy smile faltered. 'Dad's security man is here. Did you bring me a present, Aunty?'

'Not this time, dearest. I think you've got enough.' Barbra moved quickly now, moving out on to the sun-drenched deck.

Liane couldn't bring herself to talk about presents. Not now.

'There he is.' Barbra leaned over the balustrade staring down into the courtyard. 'Such an attractive young man. Just the person to accompany you and Jonathon on your long walks. You know how I hate exercise.'

'Come and meet him, Lee!' Jonathon begged. 'He's nice. He told me he'd go fishing with me. Isn't that great?'

'Yes, go down,' Barbra urged them, smiling. 'I need a few minutes to freshen up. It was a long drive.'

Barry Wiseman looked like a college student until one noticed the few lines time had traced across his forehead and around his eyes and mouth. He was tall, bone-thin, hollow-cheeked, but attractive for all that, with his lop-sided grin and firm handshake. One wouldn't know to look at him that he was an expert in karate, but he had only to move for a few seconds for the strength and grace to become apparent.

'Delighted to meet you, Mrs Wilde.' He smiled down at her, enchanted with what he saw. 'I want you to know I'll be on the job every second but I hope in the most unobtrusive way.'

'You're very welcome, Mr Wiseman.'

'Please, *Barry*. No one calls me anything fancy!'

'Really?' Julian gave him a direct thump on the shoulder. 'I can think of a few names, highly colourful.'

'That's only when I have to wear my badge.'

'Barry is ex-police force,' Julian explained. 'One of their best officers. Their loss was my gain.'

'Did you know your dad can still spring a few surprises on me when we practise our karate?' Barry looked down at Jonathon.

'Dad is strong!'

'Scary!' Barry smiled back. 'I don't think even he knows what he's capable of. He sure got you back in a hurry, and there was a team of *us*.'

They all took their leave of Julian in the courtyard.

'Come back, Dad. As soon as you can!' Jonathon hugged his father boisterously. 'I want you with me all the time.'

'I want that, too, Jonathon,' Julian assured him, 'but you mustn't forget I'm working for you. You've got a long life in front of you, and I hope you're going to spend a lot of it controlling what I build up. Wilde Holdings is for you!'

'Thanks a lot, Dad.' Jonathon hugged him gratefully. 'My headmaster thinks I'm going to be as smart as you.'

'Smarter!' Julian ruffled his son's curls. 'Take care of Liane. And your aunt.'

'Leave it to me, Dad!' Jonathon piped up gallantly. 'I'll be Barry's right-hand man.'

'Good onya, cobber,' Barry quipped laconically, obviously at ease with children.

'Goodbye, Julian!' Liane lifted her pale gold head to him, as slender as a lily in a ribbon-strapped sun-dress of finest white cotton.

For answer he tilted up her chin and to her shock gave her a brief, hard kiss on the mouth.

'Take care!' There was a devilish glint in his sapphire eyes.

'What was all that about?' Barbra demanded urgently, as they walked back into the house. Jonathon had gone along very happily to help Barry settle in and the two women were temporarily on their own. 'I do hope you're not going to allow yourself to fall back into the same old trap.'

'You don't like Julian, do you?'

'Like?' Barbra gave a brittle little laugh. 'In some ways, I really hate him. Sorry.' She caught at Liane's arm. 'I'm putting this the wrong way. Julian was married to my sister. He brought wonderful happiness and excitement into her world, then all that ceased. Caroline knew he was tiring of her. She thought the only way she could hold him was having a child. You know the rest.'

'I don't know very much at all,' Liane answered, in sudden anger. 'The subject of Julian's first marriage was always closed. I know he felt a tremendous grief at the loss of a young life.'

'Guilt, don't you mean, darling?'

Liane stopped short to stare at the older woman. 'You told me yourself Julian had no idea it was so dangerous for your sister to have a child.'

'Don't you think he should have taken the trouble to find out?'

'Surely this would have been discussed in the first place,' Liane retorted, almost heatedly. 'Julian loves children. He's very good with them. We were planning our own child. We discussed having a family before we were married.'

'Well, he would want to, wouldn't he?' said Barbra. 'He had the tragic experience of my sister. Look, I don't want to upset you, dear, this is a holiday after all, but there's a great deal you don't know about Julian. I'm older than you and far more experienced. When you married Julian you were a wide-eyed child. I remember how you looked on your wedding day. So young and exquisite it hurt. Privately I thought it was like a lamb to the slaughter, but I could hardly speak out. You were so much in love you would never have believed me anyway.'

'Believed what?' Liane gestured for Barbra to sit down in one of the blue and white upholstered cane chairs.

'Forgive me—that Julian is a dangerous man. I could see the pattern starting up all over again. My family learned the hard way. My sister was a beautiful woman, but she wasn't enough for Julian. Oh, no! Julian has always been a player of secret games. Do you know he once made a pass at me?'

Liane experienced a mad desire to scream. 'How could I, when up until now you've always kept it to yourself?'

'It was that first hot summer he and Caroline were married.'

'What?' Liane couldn't restrain her shock.

'Thank you, darling,' Barbra returned wryly, 'but I *am* considered to be a striking-looking woman.'

'Of course you are, but what you're saying sounds incredible. Julian made a pass at you when he was only just married to your sister?'

'Is it so improbable?' Barbra tossed her dark head imperiously. 'He is, without question, a highly sexed man. We were alone. We'd had a few drinks. I feel terribly sad every time I think about it, but it did happen. Of course it didn't take me long to come to my senses. Having an affair with my own sister's husband wasn't my idea of decent behaviour, but it was well and truly in Julian's mind. You must notice we're not entirely comfortable with one another. Neither of us has forgotten, you see.'

'This is a terrible shock.' On a brilliant summer's day Liane felt chilled to the bone.

'I can see that,' Barbra smiled sadly. 'I want you to know, my dear, it never happened again. I repulsed Julian so strongly I expect he has never forgiven me. The last thing I ever want you to do is repeat it. It's such an ugly story, isn't it?'

'And *evil*, if it were not true.'

'Liane, darling.' Barbra pushed back in her chair, her fine skin turning white. 'I only told you to help you. I swear that was my only motive. I'm not such a fool I can't see Julian is working to break down your defences. You only have to come into contact with the man to suffer. Julian lets nothing of his get away, even if he doesn't really want it any more.'

'And your sister, did she have any idea?'

'Good God, no!' Barbra burst out violently. 'I would never have hurt my sister for the world. We were tremendously close.'

'That's not quite right,' Liane challenged her. 'Your mother told me on one occasion you and your sister were quite different. Like chalk and cheese was the way she put it. She gave me to understand you saw very little of each other. In fact, that there had always been a sibling jealousy.'

'Families!' Barbra laughed. 'Come on now, Liane, you know families! Then again perhaps you don't. You were very much alone, weren't you? I assure you rivalry is quite common in families. It was even encouraged in ours. My mother certainly didn't give you to understand there wasn't love between us, for of course there was!'

'Except other people told me pretty much the same thing. I used to wonder about it at the time. You were always so kind and understanding with me. Julian himself appreciated it.'

'I expect he would!' Barbra's voice had a bitter tang. 'After all, you usurped my sister.'

'Oh! Please don't say that.' Liane reacted as if she had just been stabbed.

'Zeus! What a fool I am!' Barbra leant over and grasped Liane's arm. 'I don't mean it in that way. It was merely an expression. As other people might see it. I took to you at our first meeting. You had the look of an angel. A *good* girl. An innocent. I was determined to protect you. Become your big sister if you like. Even then I couldn't prevent what happened. After a while Julian went back to his old tricks. Now Lesley Bannigan was nothing! Attractive certainly, but a featherweight. Julian likes his women to have style, and that includes intelligence. Lesley Bannigan just came along. The woman you really should have been warned about was Miranda Phillips.'

'The top fashion model?' Liane asked, very sharply.

'The very one. She's working in Europe at the moment. I believe the French designers love her. She was one of the models at the spring collections. Lagerfeld, I think it was. Julian was very smitten with her. Strangely enough, she has a look of you. That blonde hair and marvellous eyes.'

'Are you telling me Julian was having an affair with Miranda Phillips too?' Liane looked at the older woman very intently.

'She never denied it when a friend of mine asked her.'

'Now that I'll never believe!' The one moment pale with shock, Liane was full of fight. 'Miranda went to primary school with me. You're right about one thing. She does look like me. People took us for sisters. She was my dearest friend. We lost contact when her father was transferred to another state but we met up again only last year. Miranda hasn't changed a bit. She even told me she knew Julian. Being so beautiful, Miranda gets invited to all the functions.'

'That she does, dear,' Barbra agreed drily. 'I know too much, you see.'

'Miranda would never do that to me! She's beautiful inside and out. Besides, I'm almost certain she was still interstate at the time.'

'Oh? So how did I know about her?'

Liane kept staring at her. 'I can check with Miranda.'

'She's bound to tell you, of course. *Yes, Liane, I did have an affair with your husband. Short but glorious.*'

'I'd have to hear that from Miranda's own lips,' Liane said loyally. 'When you look in Miranda's eyes you can see right through to her soul.'

'Enough to warp a person, I know, hearing such a thing. There is, however, a well-worn phrase: all's fair in love and war. And in Julian's case you have to add something else. He's a multi-millionaire. Women with wonderful looks generally marry rich men. Rich men can have the pick of anyone, so why would they settle for the ordinary girl who lives next door? You don't think Julian would have married you if your hair had been mousy instead of pure gold? If your skin had been poor instead of flawless? I assure you, my dear, he wouldn't have wanted you had you not been lovely to look at. You do realise that?'

'Would I have loved Julian had he not been so handsome? Yes, I expect I would. There has to be something very real behind the superficial good looks. There has to be kindness and humour and principles.'

'You said it, my dear.' Barbra turned to her, a sympathetic expression on her face. 'I rest my case.' She held up her hands like a judge.

The days passed swiftly. As long as they kept off the subject of Julian, Barbra was an easy and amusing companion, and she made a noticeable effort to better her relationship with Jonathon. The weather continued glorious, with all the physical activity instilling a feeling of health and well-being. While Barbra worked on a spectacular tan, Liane and Jonathon swam and walked and played, increasingly with Barry Wiseman in close attendance. They had come to know him well, a few short days taking him from stranger to friend. He was full of information, so the long walks turned into nature lessons about birds and trees and plants and the beautiful shells tossed up on the beach. He encouraged Jonathon to use his eyes. He even taught him new games and how to play cards, all the while maintaining a professional surveillance.

'So many sides to that young man!' Barbra observed as they watched Barry and Jonathon practising the elementary karate movements. 'I didn't think we would want him around, now I wouldn't want him to go away.'

'I liked him from the moment we met. I suppose that's always the way.'

Barbra patted her hand. 'I think he has a crush on you.'

'You're joking!' Liane felt a quick rejection.

'No, dear, I'm not. Why do you think he's making himself so charming, so talkative? Because you listen.' Barbra smiled her knowing smile. 'Worse and worse, I think he's falling in love with you.'

'How you do rave on, Barbra.'

'Liane, darling,' Barbra said archly, 'you know as well as I do he finds you very, very attractive.'

'And I *like* him,' Liane confirmed, looking out over the white sand to the rolling surf beyond, 'but that's a long way from the nonsense you're talking.'

'Is it?' Barbra tipped her wide-brimmed straw hat further over her eyes. 'Just watch him at dinner. He notices every little thing about you. How you wear a flower in your hair. Everything you put on. He's strongly attracted to you, and I suppose he wishes he weren't. Think what Julian might do if an employee fell in love with his ex-wife? I think I've stressed before that Julian is the most aggressive of men.'

Liane very firmly changed the subject, but Barbra had planted the seeds of uncertainty. The flower in her hair at dinner had started with Jonathon's delight. The small boy remembered the golden days of Sandpiper, the days of Liane's marriage when Julian often broke off a flower and tucked it into his wife's hair. That evening Liane found herself pinning two perfect gardenias behind one ear, so that her hair fell in a one-sided ash-gold curtain. Her skin had taken on a light gold sheen which had the effect of lightening her hair and darkening her eyes. They were neither green nor azure, but an ever-changing mix of both. Although there was always the most beautiful sea breeze, the nights were hot enough to keep clothing to a minimum. Both Barbra and Liane had taken to dressing in gorgeously printed sarongs wrapped gracefully around the body and leaving the arms and shoulders bare. Barbra had found them in a resort boutique and bought a collection because the fabrics used were so beautiful and they were a breeze to wear.

Tonight Liane put on her favourite luminous pinks, blues, greens and citrus yellows on a white ground. Barbra had been so good to give them to her. Not only were they fun and easy to wear, they could be made to look extremely dressy. Barbra, for instance, always wore hers with loads of imaginative resort jewellery, her dark golden tan and dark colouring giving her the appearance of an island princess. Liane on the other hand kept her throat bare, relying on the lovely flowers Jonathon chose from the garden as her only adornment. Had she only known it, it was more than enough. Liane had never placed a great deal of emphasis on her natural good looks. They were there. Normal.

In the middle of a delicious dinner served out on the deck, Liane suddenly became aware Barry was staring at her. Always when they were together, Barry's manner and conversation was that of a cousin. Warm and friendly but certainly platonic. The look she intercepted gave her pause. It was deeply admiring, as though her beauty gave him great pleasure.

'What's up?' The voice was Barbra's, cheerful but ever so slightly mocking.

'Forgive me, was I staring?' The unflappable Barry blushed.

'I thought you were going to say something.' Liane tried to help him out.

'I'll bet he was: he likes your sarong. It really does suit you, Liane.' Barbra smiled at her with long, glittering eyes. 'I'm so glad I bought them. You've no idea how piquant a sarong looks on a golden blonde.'

'Dad always says Lee looks like a mermaid, but I think she looks like Rose White in my old story book,' Jonathon piped up. 'I'll show it to you afterwards, Barry,' he offered. 'She looks just like Lee.'

'How you do turn the men's heads,' Barbra said indulgently, pushing back her chair. 'I'll say this for Rosa, she's a superb cook. If I'm not careful I'll put on weight.'

'You should come for a walk with us,' Barry suggested with a touch sarcasm of his own. 'Walking is the best exercise of all.'

'I know, dear boy, but I'm hopelessly lazy. If I have to lose weight, it's by dieting, not getting physical. Sorry, but that's the way I am.'

'Not that you ever have a problem,' Liane pointed out quickly, aware of a slight edginess in the air. 'I've never seen you other than beautifully slim.'

'*I* think so,' Barbra said. 'And, so saying, I think I'll have just a teensy weensy slice of that marvellous chocolate torte. I simply can't resist chocolate, can you?'

No one answered her. A curious restraint had entered the atmosphere. Even Jonathon in his sensitivity divined a change of mood. Relationships always reached a point where certain things occurred. In the case of men and women, friendship and admiration could often turn to love. Nevertheless, after dinner, the three of them went for their customary short walk. Barbra from the beginning had cried off, preferring to listen to music under the stars. Liane had not realised Barbra was a fairly heavy drinker. Indeed she derived a great deal of pleasure from plundering Nick de Lucca's superbly stocked cellar. Liane thought she would have to mention this to Julian. Barbra invariably finished off the wine when they went for their after-dinner walk, or if that was finished she called for more. Much as Nick de Lucca had given instructions to keep his guests happy, Liane was starting to worry that they were overstepping the mark.

A strong breeze was blowing in from the ocean, making Liane's hair whip around her face.

'Isn't this marvellous?' Jonathon called delightedly, running before them. 'See, Lee and Barry, there's the Southern Cross. It's right over the house. It's so easy to count the points. Oh, I love the beach!'

'There's little fear he won't put his bad experience behind him,' Barry confided to Liane in a quiet undertone. 'He's a great little fellow. I know I've never met such a bright kid. He's so aware.'

'Yes, he is,' Liane agreed. 'I never thought he would keep me in his heart. He was only four when Julian and I separated. Such a *little* boy, I thought, in fact I hoped for his sake he would forget me, but he didn't at all. I'll never forget that night Julian brought him back. He opened his eyes and smiled at me. He didn't have the least difficulty knowing who I was, and he was drugged.'

'I think anyone would find it difficult to forget you,' Barry said in a deep voice. 'Please forgive me if I presume on our friendship, but I simply can't understand how you and Julian parted. I've come to know Julian very well. It seems to me once Julian decided he loved a woman, nothing on earth would change that. His feelings run very deep. The things that matter are tremendously important to him.'

'I would have thought so, Barry.'

'Yet you are divorced?'

'Yes.'

'I can't understand it,' Barry repeated. 'Julian couldn't find a more beautiful woman if he searched the earth. You're so sweet and gentle with everyone. Jonathon adores you.'

'Jonathon is why I'm here.'

Barry gazed down at her from his superior height. 'Are you telling me you and Julian will remain divorced?'

'Why are you asking, Barry?' Liane held her hair away from her face.

'I would really like to know.'

'I can't tell you what I don't know myself. No one who has ever known Julian is free of him. Least of all me. He has so much charisma. His fascination is endless.'

'But we're not discussing fascination. Julian is *real*. He's a very real, masterful man. I don't suppose I should be saying this, but Barbra has it in for him, hasn't she?'

'Why do you say that?' Liane asked him, unable to ignore Barry's sharp perceptions.

'It's the way she handles everything. The way she handles you. I'm probably speaking out of turn. I know you see her as your friend, but Barbra is one deeply troubled lady. On the one hand she's so confident, assertive; on the other I think she sees herself as deprived. She's one heck of a good-looking woman, if you like the type, yet she remains unmarried.'

'Marriage isn't the key to happiness, Barry,' Liane pointed out wryly.

'I realise that, but what I'm saying is, most people do *try* it. The only other option is to go it alone, and most people don't want to do that. Especially women. Being on her own would restrict her in the social sphere, wouldn't it? I believe Kate Stafford, the heiress, only remarried to gain herself an escort. A man on his own can get invited everywhere, but it's not so easy for a mature woman alone.'

'Barbra is never short of a party to join,' Liane explained carefully. 'She has always been on the social scene. Everyone knows her.'

'It's strange all the same,' Barry persisted. 'In my opinion Barbra is material for a book. Her little digs at

Julian would seem to stress her veiled hostility, but have you ever noticed her eyes when his name is mentioned? They get fixated. There's a lot of conflict locked away in her. I know it sounds weird, but I have a theory she's secretly in love with him. Maybe she has never been able to express it, Julian being married to her sister and all that. It must be rather awful living with a perceived taboo. Maybe she refused to allow her deepest feelings to develop. As a character study, she interests me. For one, there's Julian. For another, there's you. You know she sees herself in competition with you?'

'In what way?' Liane tried to keep the agitation out of her voice.

'In every way.' Barry gazed down at her pale gold head. 'I suppose a good-looking woman would fight getting older. I know it drives her nuts you're so beautiful.'

'Oh, nonsense,' Liane said fretfully. 'Barbra is a very striking woman. Why should she ever feel threatened by me?'

'Are you going to listen?' Barry asked quietly.

'You sound worried, Barry.' Liane tilted her head to look at him.

'I must admit I am, a little. Nothing is as it seems. Barbra is here as your friend, yet my intuition, my training, tells me she's not your friend at all. That doesn't make for a good situation. For one thing, it restricts you in your dealings with her. I've thought about this very carefully. Believe me, I know my place, but I'm concerned for you. Moreover, Julian is my friend as well as my employer. Julian feels very strongly about you, whatever you feel about him. Barbra is using everything she's got, and she's clever. Most of the time she sounds normal and friendly, then she slips in her fleeting, unsettling little comments. She works overtime to ensure you and Julian remain apart. All this rubbish about Julian chasing women. Nothing could be further from the truth, and I should know because I'm with him most of the time. In the two years I've worked for him Julian has been totally committed to expanding his business empire. He only has to show up at a function for five minutes and the photographers grab some good-looking female to pose with him. Julian is centre-stage. That's why he gets so much exposure. He's a truly glamorous human being. He's better-looking than Mel Gibson and he's a great achiever. Women just naturally surround him. Men, too, only they don't bother photographing him with all the guys. Sometimes I'd like to smash a few cameras to protect him. The Press are *insatiable*. They can ruin lives too. I've heard Barbra's little cracks about Julian and I've seen how they affect you. What I want to say is this: don't place much credence in what Barbra tells you.'

'And you've divined all this in under a week?' Liane gave a little self-derisive laugh.

'Sometimes we are blind to the people closest to us. I know Barbra likes to play Big Sister with you, superior worldly experience and all that, but I'm becoming anxious that she tries to create complications. For instance, she has noticed what is happening to me and she's trying to make it work for her.'

'I'm not following you, Barry.'

'I think you are. I'll only speak of this once and never again. Had things been quite different, perhaps, I could have allowed myself to fall in love with you. As it is, I can't repress my pleasure in your company but I *can* repress my thoughts and actions. For better or worse, I believe you think of yourself as Julian's wife. I know you are never out of *his* mind. I sympathise with both of you. And myself. There are not, and never will be, bad intentions on my part. I respect all three of us too much. Now that's over, I'll only add one more thing. Barbra is trying to mastermind a romance. I know she has said something to you and she has hinted to me. It's all related to her own goals. I think she'd like to tell Julian we've become very close; imply much, much more than our friendship. I don't think she'd give a damn if I lost a valued and highly paid job, but that's not the main aim. In my view, it's to keep you and Julian apart.'

'Perhaps she's obsessively protective,' Liane suggested ironically.

'I think her feeling for Julian is central to everything. No matter what she says, that feeling is intense.'

'Of course you're right!' Liane sighed.

'I like to think I'm a bit of an amateur psychologist, and a lot of police work helps. One has to deal with so many people who split themselves into multiple personalities. I thought about this a good deal before I spoke. In his absence, Julian has given me the role of protector. It's fitting I should keep my eye on Miss Edwards. My internal voice tells me she's an habitual troublemaker, and her curious hostility towards Julian sets her apart. Forgive me if I upset you, but I don't see her as your friend. In my own case I feel she's working to portray me as the man who has spent the entire week trying to win his employer's wife.'

'Ex-wife, Barry. I went to a great deal of pain and trouble to secure a divorce.'

'But you didn't *want* it, did you?'

Liane shook her head. 'I thought Julian no longer wanted me. I couldn't live with that, Barry.'

'You thought he had abandoned you for another woman. Tell me to mind my own business whenever you want to, but I'd really like to help. I've seen enough of Barbra to realise she's quite capable of poisoning minds. I think she's had a lot of experience doing it. I wouldn't like to hear it was Barbra who told you what she thought Julian was doing.'

'Barbra didn't come into it at all.'

'Are you sure of that?'

'It was someone entirely different. Barbra was marvellously supportive. Afterwards.'

'Then I can't begin to fathom it.' Barry scratched his thick sandy thatch. 'One hears all the gossip, as you can well imagine, and the gossipmongers make Julian suffer. I wish to go on record here and now and say I consider him to be the straightest man I have ever known. He has a fixed belief that you are still his wife. For a man who was supposed to be unfaithful he has a remarkable capacity for single-mindedness. Love is expressed not by words but by actions. Don't you think his allegiance to you is extreme for a man who is supposed to be drawn to other women?'

'I wish I knew.'

'And there you run up against Julian's pride,' Barry pointed out gently. 'I suppose, in a general way, if you're not with Julian, you're against him. For the most important person in his life to doubt him would raise tremendous barriers.'

'He never has forgiven me, if that's what you mean. He believes I should have trusted him no matter how many people...'

'...tried to frame him?' Barry interjected. 'People do it all the time. In large numbers. Women, especially, are very good at it. These days Julian is rarely out of my sight, yet he was supposed to have had a thing going with Vanessa Shepherd. You may have seen something in the gossip columns. They left me out of the photographs. I was usually on the other side. The media are in constant need of gossip to feed their readers. People in the limelight have a terrible time. The only thing they can do is deny the rumours and grow a tough skin. It's not easy. Everyone is entitled to a private life.'

'You really are Julian's friend, aren't you?'

'He inspires loyalty.'

'And you feel I may have let him down?'

'I didn't say that, Liane,' Barry denied uncomfortably. 'I only wish I had have been around at the time. I was a pretty good detective in my day. Just for the record, what was the woman's name?'

'Surely you've heard it?'

'Didn't take it in. That was before I met you. She wasn't a member of Barbra's circle?'

'As a matter of fact she was, but Barbra says they were never close. I'm speaking to you in confidence, Barry. Her name was Lesley Bannigan.'

'Good lord!' Barry said, with some caution.

'Yes, the Bannigans split up, but not before Julian put him out of business. Julian does have a ruthless side.'

'I expect you don't know he has since tried to make amends? Bannigan doesn't hold anything against him.'

'There was no doubt, Barry,' Liane said very quietly. 'Lesley Bannigan came to me and told me everything. She had nothing to gain. In fact she had everything to lose. As it happened, her husband.'

'I still feel there's something wrong,' Barry replied.

'None of us know all there is to know about another person. We don't even know what's hidden inside ourselves. I can't go back to the blind faith I had. At the moment I have no answers at all, but I do need a friend.'

'Then you have one,' Barry assured her. 'Be sure I will never presume beyond that.'

Just when it seemed they would have another quiet, relaxing day Rosa came rushing down the winding stairs and on to the beach.

'Mrs Wilde!'

'Rosa wants you, Lee!' Jonathon broke away from his game to run up to Liane as she lay sunning on the beach. 'She looks like she's in a hurry.'

Liane sat up quickly and slipped on her beach coat.

'A visitor, Madam. Sir Eric Mossleigh.'

'What!' Jonathon's small face showed a ludicrous disgust. 'What's he doing here? He can't come here. He's not allowed.'

'What is it, Liane?' Barry loped up to them, his indolence swiftly discarded.

'I'm sure I don't know. It's my boss, Sir Eric Mossleigh. I never thought he would come here. Where's Barbra?'

'She's speaking to him now, madam.' Rosa was faintly agitated. 'It seems she forgot to tell you he was coming.'

'And how did she know?' Barry frowned.

'It seems she took a phone call when you were on the beach last evening.'

'And she forgot to tell you?' Barry looked directly into Liane's troubled eyes. 'That's a bit much to swallow.'

'Thank you, Rosa,' Liane managed pleasantly. 'I'll come up now and I'll use the side entrance so that I can get dressed. Would you mind very much making Sir Eric tea while he's waiting? Black, no sugar.'

'Well, what do you think of that?' Jonathon asked them in round-eyed amazement. 'Are you going to tell him to go, Barry? Dad wouldn't want him here.'

'It's Liane's decision, old man.'

'You don't want him here, do you, Lee?' Jonathon asked incredulously.

Liane shook her head.

'Neither do I, and neither does Barry. I think I'll ring Dad.'

'Jonathon, come back!' Liane called as Jonathon started to run off. 'I can handle this. Sir Eric is my boss!'

'What does he want to talk to you about when you're on holiday?' Jonathon fought his rebellion.

'Now that I shall have to find out. Please stay here with Barry.'

'We'll be up in about an hour.' Barry took a firm hold of Jonathon's hand. 'If you need us any sooner, get Rosa to wave from the deck.'

'He's a nice man, Barry,' Liane tried to reassure him. 'Sir Eric has been very good to me.'

'Then one must suppose he wants something,' Barry said tartly.

When Liane hurried down to the living-room dressed in narrow slacks with a hand-painted silk top, Barbra and Sir Eric were seated on a long sofa facing the ocean. They were deep in conversation and Liane stopped, thinking she would like to have been a fly on the wall. What did Barbra and Sir Eric have in common to be so serious about? They were so intent on their conversation, they had not noticed her arrival in the doorway.

'Good morning, Eric,' Liane said calmly and walked into the big, luxurious room.

'Ah, good morning my dear.' Instantly Sir Eric rose to his feet, his pleasure softening the sharpness of his expression. 'I gather Barbra forgot to tell you I was going to be in the area.'

'As a matter of fact, she did,' Liane said amicably, giving nothing away. 'No matter, it's lovely to see you.'

'And you, my dear.' Sir Eric came to her, bending his silver-winged head and kissing her on the cheek. 'You look marvellous. A sun-tan with your hair and eyes is extraordinary.'

'That's what I tell her,' Barbra announced gaily, springing up. 'Now I'll leave you two alone. I'm sure you have lots to talk about.'

'Alex and I were taking a look at some acreage near Paradise Valley,' Sir Eric explained. 'De Lucca Constructions, of course. How that man has prospered since your ex-husband took an interest in him. How is the boy?'

Liane gestured for Sir Eric to sit down. 'He's doing very well. We're keeping his body and mind so occupied he hasn't had time to dwell on his experience. Getting away was the right idea.'

'I've missed you dreadfully!' Sir Eric said.

'Surely Miss McKay is very competent.'

'You know what I mean, my dear.' Sir Eric fixed her with his penetrating gaze. 'How much longer does Wilde expect you to sacrifice your life?'

'You don't understand, Eric. It's no sacrifice. I love Jonathon. He has made a great recovery but I would like to see him through another month.'

'Another month?' Sir Eric appeared devastated. 'My dear, I can't spare you for that.'

'Then I must ask you to accept my resignation.'

Sir Eric didn't even bother to conceal his swift anger. 'I'd be glad to!' he said tersely. 'Surely you know I don't want you in the workplace? I want you for my wife!'

He sounded so painfully emphatic that Liane's tender heart smote her. 'That's impossible, Eric,' she said unhappily. 'I am very grateful to you for all that you have done for me, but I simply don't love you. I have never thought to love you.'

'Surely you don't think what is happening now with Wilde is better?'

'What *is* happening?' Liane asked tautly. 'Please explain.'

'Miss Edwards tells me he's up to his old tricks.'

'And what would Barbra know?'

'Liane, my dear, she's his sister-in-law. She must know a great deal.'

'And you were the one who told me she once had an interest in Julian herself.'

'I was mistaken about that.'

'Did she put you straight?'

'My dear, please don't get angry at your friends. We're only trying to protect you.'

'I'm working on protecting myself. I'm not the innocent I once was. I believed what my *friends* told me. Now I'm likely to consider *why* they told me. In Barbra's case, perhaps she wanted to wreck my marriage. If she did, I certainly left myself open to a destructive influence. In your case, you told me yourself you wanted me years ago. I've been associated with you long enough to know you're a long-range planner.'

'What has turned you against me?' Sir Eric cried. 'I swear to you my every action has been completely honest and above board. I had absolutely nothing to do with the break-up of your marriage. Surely you believe that?'

'I don't know what to believe any more. Maybe I'm a late developer. It's only now I'm beginning to question these so-called pure motives. May I ask you a question?'

'Why, certainly, my dear. Anything!'

'What were you and Barbra talking about when I walked in?'

Sir Eric's black brows beetled. 'I'm not sure.'

'What would you and Barbra have to talk about so intently? You were quite engrossed.'

'Why, you, of course.' Sir Eric did not drop his unwinking gaze.

'I can't believe you were talking about me. I have the certain feeling it was something quite different. One thing I do have to recognise in myself is, I am very sensitive to atmosphere. You and Barbra were talking about... *business.*'

'That's ridiculous,' Sir Eric scoffed. 'No disrespect to Miss Edwards, but I don't think she would know a thing about it.'

'Except I saw your expression. It's one I know very well. It's the look you get on your face when you're considering your moves. Don't forget I've worked for you for two years.'

'My dearest Liane, you're quite wrong. Would I lie to you?'

'Of course you would.' Liane laughed abruptly. 'I don't wish to offend you, but you know you would lie to me if the truth put you or your ventures at risk. The thing is, what could Barbra possibly tell you?'

'Liane, that's enough of this,' Sir Eric said crisply. 'I think this new suspicion has more to do with Wilde's coming back into your life. Your friend, Miss Edwards, is concerned for you. You talk about my being a planner, a master wheeler-dealer! Why, Wilde could give *me* lessons. Nobody knows for sure if he didn't put that damned woman and her son up to snatching the boy just to get you to come back to him.'

Liane looked her distaste. 'For a brilliant man, that's positively stupid.'

'How you have changed!' Sir Eric observed ironically.

'You don't like me with my eyes open?'

'Liking has nothing to do with love. We can like hundreds of people through the years, but in my experience love is possible only once.'

'Perhaps you're right.'

'And I don't mean Wilde! Wilde was your Svengali. You were just a child. Won't you allow yourself time, Liane? You owe me nothing, but I'd dearly love you to get to know me.'

'Eric!'

'Please,' he insisted. 'Let me show you what being in my world would be like. I could give you everything. You're so beautiful I could shower you with jewels and furs and clothes. Surely you're woman enough to want to own fabulous things?'

'I did own fabulous things,' Liane pointed out quietly. 'I sent them back.'

'You expected something of Wilde that he can't give. His total fidelity. I can. I know what that means to you. What it would mean to any woman who values her self-respect. I've come here today simply because I couldn't stay away.'

'Are you sure it wasn't to see Barbra?' Liane surprised herself.

'Dearest girl, how you shock me. You have never been cynical before.'

'I shall be in future. Being naïve could have ruined two years of my life. It changed the lives of three people: Julian, Jonathon, myself.'

Sir Eric stiffened. 'Forgive me if I'm not surprised. Wilde is celebrated for his mesmeric effect on women. He only has to lift a finger and they come running. What's in store for you if he takes you back into his life? Do you really think he won't follow the same old pattern? Temporarily you might be happy, then he'll take his little breaks. The years will bring total disenchantment. They could even lead to a profound loneliness. You'll sacrifice your friends to keep Wilde. I can't stand by and see that happen.'

'And that's the problem. I've been allowing other people to run my life. I'm not such a poor thing I can't find a life outside Julian. I think all of us must reach a point when we have to face reality. If Julian and I are incompatible in matters of conduct and I've chosen to believe his enemies, I'll have to live with it. But you must understand my nature. I could not marry without love. I could not give myself to a man I did not love with all my heart. I know other women make arrangements in life, and perhaps those arrangements work for them, but not for me. I admire and respect you, Eric, but I cannot marry you. It would be a crime to allow you to think I might change my mind.'

'My dear, you haven't yet encountered the very real problems in life,' Sir Eric pointed out harshly. 'There is the matter of supporting yourself. Regrettably, under the circumstances I could not take you back as my secretary. You've long been accustomed to a high standard of living. I would not be your friend if I did not voice a few cautions. You're twenty-six. High time you re-married. I note you love your ex-husband's child, but you're leaving having your own child too long. The older a woman gets, the greater the risks. Soon you'll be thirty. It's easy to talk now about what you're going to do, but will you think the same in even a few years? I am offering you a secure life. I am offering you my total devotion. With a little less rigidity on your part I am certain you could come to love me. Wilde has alienated us and he'll pay for it!'

Barry and Jonathon stood hand in hand on the decking watching Sir Eric's chauffeur-driven Rolls speed off.

'Gosh, he left in a hurry!' Jonathon exclaimed in some awe. 'We were just coming to throw him out, weren't we, Barry?'

'Your idea, pal, not mine.'

'Was that Sir Eric's car?' Barbra rushed out on to the deck, flinging out a staying arm.

'Of course!' Jonathon looked up at his aunt as though she were stupid. 'Why didn't you tell us he was coming? Lee was cross.'

'Because, my darling, I forgot!' Barbra's dark eyes were filled with dismay. 'The phone call simply went out of my head.'

'How is that possible?' Liane turned to face her.

Barbra's expression was pained. 'Haven't you ever forgotten a phone message, dear? If you hadn't gone down to the beach so early, I'm certain I would have remembered it.'

'Dad'll be spitting chips.' Jonathon announced with some satisfaction.

'You shouldn't say that!' Barbra protested. 'Really, Liane, Jonathon is getting a little out of hand.'

Jonathon was leaning back against Liane and she smoothed his hair. 'He's speaking the simple truth. Julian would be very angry if he knew Eric had come here. I'm very surprised he did, or did he really come to see you?'

'My dear girl!' Barbra looked stunned. 'Are you sure you haven't had too much sun? Eric Mossleigh is certainly not in love with me.'

Jonathon swivelled his curly dark head and looked up at Liane helplessly. 'Is that old man in love with you?'

'Darling, that's not very nice! Sir Eric is not old.'

'That's not what Dad says. He said he's going to wipe the old devil out.'

'I think that's enough for today.' Liane halted the conversation. 'If Barry is going to take us to the lighthouse you have some reading to catch up on, and a page of spelling.'

'I know it already,' Jonathon said dismissively, looking up at Liane. 'I don't want him to ever come here again.'

'I don't think he will, dear.' Liane looked suddenly very young and vulnerable. 'Besides, did I tell you he sacked me?'

# CHAPTER SIX

JULIAN'S secretary rang on the Friday morning to say that Mr Wilde would be unable to make the trip that weekend and would be ringing himself later in the day.

Jonathon banged the breakfast table with his spoon. 'You mean Dad isn't going to be here after all?'

'Good lord, Jonathon!' Barry protested, and took the spoon off him. 'Your father is a very important man. He can't always get away when he wants to, but he will be speaking to you today. He'll probably come later in the week.'

'Excuses, excuses!' Barbra breathed lightly. 'Julian isn't the best father in the world.'

'He is, he is!' Jonathon shouted wildly, pushing back his chair and charging from the room.

'Did you *really* have to say that, Barbra?' Liane asked in distress. 'It was cruel and completely untrue.'

Barbra did not apologise. She kept hold of her coffee-cup, smiling thinly. 'The demands of big business is one of the best excuses a man can have. I don't expect I have to tell *you* that!'

It was the third upset of the morning. Liane pushed back her chair only fractionally less tempestuously than Jonathon and went after him. He was out on the terrace, racing a small car furiously across the tiles. He had tears in his eyes.

'Come here to me,' Liane called. 'I know you're a big man but come here to me all the same.'

Jonathon jumped up immediately, wiping his cheeks with the back of his hand. 'I really hate Aunty Barbra. I feel like telling her to get lost.'

'I have to admit she does come on too strong.' Liane wrapped her arms around him, upset at the shaking in his small body. 'I'm a bit angry at her myself. It's just her way, Jonathon. Some people express themselves in a sarcastic manner.'

'Yeah,' Jonathon said disgustedly. 'She talks about Dad, yet she's over at our place all the time. Don't you think that's strange?'

'She comes to see you.'

Jonathon drew back his head, staring at her for a long moment with his big blue eyes. 'She says she does, but it doesn't feel like it. She sure doesn't speak to me much of the time. She's always grabbing hold of Dad's arm and saying silly things.'

'Like what?' Liane asked with some difficulty.

'I forget,' Jonathon said solemnly. 'But I know they're silly at the time. She reminds me of that Joy woman who often stops off to say hello to Dad. It drives me mad!'

'Well, simmer down now,' Liane begged him. 'We're having such a lovely time. Don't let anything spoil it. I'll speak to Barbra and you can speak to your father when he rings. I'm sure he wanted to come, Jonathon, but sometimes these things aren't easy to manage. He hinted he was into some big venture.'

'I expect so.' Jonathon's resentment quickly faded. 'Barry says I should be very glad to have my Dad. He's brilliant.'

'He is!' Liane seconded wryly. Most women would have settled for a true-blue guy!

By mid-week Julian still hadn't arrived, and Barbra encouraged them to go on a day trip to the mountains they had been talking about. 'I'd come with you, only I feel a bad head coming on. Probably too much sun.'

'I think it's too late,' Liane ventured, 'it's almost lunch time already.'

'Oh, please, Lee,' Jonathon begged her, hugging her around the neck. 'Let's go. We can get something to eat on the way.'

'Then we'd better ask Barry.' Liane rose to her feet. 'He's the boss.'

'Wouldn't he like to be!' Barbra murmured slyly after Jonathon had moved off. 'He's yours, that young man, any time you want him.'

'Please don't interfere, Barbra,' Liane said almost sadly. 'Maybe you don't realise what damage a careless tongue can do.'

'Oh, come off it, Liane!' Barbra said sharply. 'You will adopt this holier-than-thou attitude. You know damn well Barry is in love with you. No, don't deny it. His feeling for you runs through everything he says and does. As far as I'm concerned, you can captivate the whole male sex if you want to. It's Julian who's the threat.'

'How can Julian threaten me?' Liane asked, looking at the older woman steadily. 'I'm wondering if I wasted my time and money altogether getting a divorce. So far as you're all concerned I'm still Mrs Julian Wilde.'

'Have you never thought all that would end, if you remarried? What are you waiting for, Liane? Prince Charming won't come along. He's a fairy-tale anyway. You have two highly eligible men eating out of your hand, Eric Mossleigh and now Barry Wiseman. I wouldn't expect you to be smart enough to grab dear old Eric.'

'Thank you, Barbra,' Liane said drily. 'You must have been playing me for a fool all along.'

The irony of her tone made Barbra sit up quickly in her deckchair. 'Hey, darling, take it easy. It seems I have to be very careful around you these days. You're so *quick* to take offence. All I meant was, that high moral code of yours is preventing you from making a brilliant match. You'd think marrying one of the richest men in the country was a complete drag.'

'I should think it would be frightful getting into bed with a man I didn't love, and that's what it comes down to. I wouldn't be always sitting at the other end of the dinner table.'

'Actually he's a fine-looking man,' Barbra mused. 'I don't think there would be any inexpert fumblings. I'd say the old devil knows what he's about.'

'Then why don't *you* go after him?' Liane couldn't resist asking.

'Me?' Barbra looked up at her with long, gleaming eyes. 'He's not interested in me, dear. Ruthless men go after little white lambs. It makes them feel good. They can use that when they're up to their necks in crooked deals. No, no, dear, the best way to seduce a man is with soft, gentle ways. Make them think you need them desperately to look after you. You're very feminine, aren't you, as opposed to *femme fatale*, and God knows you're that too. If I didn't like you so much, I'd be happy to see you drown.'

'Then I'll be sure to take care in the water,' Liane answered, very drily. 'I don't know what time we'll be home exactly, but it should be before dark.'

'Take all the time you want,' Barbra told her cheerfully. 'I'll be perfectly all right.'

Their day in the hinterland was the ultimate in spectacular scenery and unalloyed delight. Barbra was not there to unsettle them with her talk. They had a late lunch at a beautiful mountain resort, then went for a long walk through a sanctuary of great flowering trees and soaring palms and ferns. Everything was so moist and luxuriantly green it was like being in Eden surrounded by emerald ferns and mosses with glittering cascades of water streaming over the tiered rockface. It was impossible to move through such beauty without feeling enriched.

As usual, Barry was a storehouse of information, identifying trees and the variety of lovely ferns, even the piercingly beautiful voices of birds high up in the grand canopy of the emerald forest.

'How did you learn all this, Barry?' Liane asked him, her voice soft in keeping with the beautiful cathedral atmosphere.

'From my Dad,' Barry explained simply. 'He lived for the outdoors; astride a horse, hunting, observing wildlife. He started off with a dairy farm in New Zealand then he brought us all over to Australia. He thought Australia was the most exciting place to be. It's so *big*, and there are still huge tracts of wilderness undisturbed by man. I suppose Australia is the last frontier, and there's so much freedom. Whenever Dad went out on his trips, I went along. He taught me so many things I have never forgotten. He was full of vigour and humour.'

'He's no longer alive?'

'He got the craze for rock-climbing when other men decide to stay at home and play bowls. Mum knew, but as always she felt she had to let him have fun. Eventually, after an ambitious climb, he didn't come home. All in all, I suppose it was the way he wanted to go.'

'I'm sorry.' Liane reached out and touched Barry's hand.

'His spirit is still around.' Barry's smile was crooked. He looked down at her slender hand over his then immediately spoke briskly. 'Now, we'd better not let Jonathon get too far ahead. He has more than a touch of adventurer in him, I'll be thinking!'

Under normal circumstances they would have arrived home in the late afternoon, but Barry stopped to help a young couple in trouble with their car. Although he knew immediately what was wrong and how to fix it, progress was rather slow and they came down the mountain to a breathtaking sunset.

'That was a marvellous day, Barry, thank you!' Liane said dreamily.

'I had no idea it was getting so late.'

'You were too busy playing the Good Samaritan. Anyway, there's no problem. I'm quite happy to settle for a sandwich after that delightful lunch, and I don't think Jonathon has much room left. Mrs Morona can have the evening off if she likes.'

'Don't forget Aunty Barbra!' Jonathon warned from the back seat. 'Aunty Barbra likes a drink.'

By the time they arrived back it was quite dark. They stood in the courtyard laughing at Jonathon's sleepy antics before Barry parked the car in a garage that served four vehicles and a boat.

Suddenly the courtyard was flooded with light and they all looked up to see two people standing on the upper deck. One was Barbra, the other...

'Dad!' Jonathon yelled, in an ecstasy of excitement.

'It's Julian!' Liane shook back her long hair. 'I'd better go up.'

'I think he has something on his mind,' Barry said quietly. 'Maybe Barbra has set us all up for a lecture.'

'That's OK,' Liane answered spiritedly. 'I'm just about set to throw her out.'

'Well, we won't jump to conclusions yet,' Barry warned, lifting his long arm to give his boss a wave.

Julian's answering salute was brief and he made no attempt to call down to them.

'Good old Miss Snoopy,' Barry hissed and walked away.

As Liane walked out on to the deck, Jonathon was hugging his father, his small arms locked behind Julian's neck. 'Dad, oh, Dad, it's so great to see you. You've arrived in time for dinner.'

Julian appeared to be unusually serious, his handsome face set in its daunting cast. Nevertheless he ran his hand over his son's head. 'You look wonderful. As fit as a fiddle.'

'Surprise, surprise, Barry took us up to the mountains today. We went for a long walk through the forest and Barry told us all the names. There was a beautiful waterfall.'

'I'm glad you enjoyed it. Barry is being very kind to you.'

'Barry's great!' Jonathon's face shone. 'Ask Lee.'

'How are you, Julian?' Liane walked towards him, her manner as subdued as his.

'Liane.' He made no attempt to kiss her and she did not extend her hand. 'You must have spent quite a few hours in the sun.'

Her eyes sparkled like jewels in her pale gold face. 'Am I to take it you don't like my tan?'

'As a matter of fact you look exquisite, as I'm sure you've been told.'

She sighed very deeply, knowing her feeling of apprehension was right. 'Darling,' she said to Jonathon briskly, 'why don't you run in and say hello to Mrs Morona? Tell her your father is having dinner with us.'

'But she must know?'

'Tell her all the same, then you can go upstairs. I'll follow in a moment to run your bath. You can spend the rest of the evening with your father.'

'OK, Lee,' said Jonathon happily. 'This is the best part of a wonderful day.'

'I was getting concerned you were so late.' Barbra, who had been standing silently in the shadows, suddenly came forward to join them.

'Why is that, Barbra?' Liane returned in a crisp voice. 'You knew the time we left.'

'Even so, darling,' Barbra looked back at her amused, 'I did expect you before dark.'

'Please don't worry about me, Barbra. I can take care of myself.'

'You're turning into quite a woman!' Barbra laughed. 'Now, as you are home safely, I'll go and dress for dinner. It has all been terribly informal, Julian, with you away. Liane and I have been living in sarongs, of all things. Let's face it, Liane looks good in anything, but you should see her in a sarong! It has practically sealed Barry's downfall.'

'Barbra!' Liane cried, shocked and disgusted.

'Just having a little fun, dear. You have nothing to look so guilty about.'

'There's more than a hint of bitch in Barbra!' Liane said between small, clenched teeth. 'It's about time I thought of giving her the boot.'

'So *aggressive*!' Julian looked down his arrogant nose at her. 'I find Barbra a veritable mine of information.'

'If I were you,' Liane retorted angrily, 'I'd close the mine down. How are you, Julian? I see you're wearing your black tyrant's face.'

'It seems a tragedy I've come back to break things up.'

'*What* things?' In her anger and protectiveness towards Barry she came close to him grasping his arm.

'This is interesting!' drawled Julian hatefully. 'The Persian kitten has become a tigress.'

'Count on it!' Her iridescent eyes flashed. 'So you've been trading information with Barbra?'

'Surely that's what you've been doing with Mossleigh?'

'I beg your pardon!' Liane threw up her ash-gold head.

'He was here?' Julian asked dauntingly.

'Not at my invitation.'

'Of course not.' The disturbing mouth thinned. 'I don't intend to stage a battle out here on the deck. Would you mind coming into the study.'

'Yes, I do! I'm not one of your unfortunate employees. You're not putting me on the mat.'

'Perhaps you'd prefer I talk to Barry?'

'Barry's too good for you,' she flared.

He looked at her coldly, his blue eyes with the glint of ice. 'That wasn't very bright of you.'

'So, do you sack him?'

'No,' he returned harshly, 'I'll simply remove him from this cosy environment.'

'Julian!' She stared up at him, her flawless skin paling beneath her light golden tan.

'Come with me.' He took hold of her authoritatively and ushered her in silence through the living-room and along to the study where he not only closed the door but locked it.

He was wearing a dark business suit, striped shirt and silk tie and he looked very polished and ruthless at the same time.

'What is it? What is it you want to ask me?' In her agitation she put her hands to her hair trying unsuccessfully to draw it into a loose knot. Her diaphanous sherbet-coloured blouse had slipped a large pearly button in her mock struggles with Jonathon and now it revealed the tender, shadowed cleft between her breasts. Even her narrow jeans were body-hugging, and she looked very young and beautiful and somewhat disarrayed. Obviously he found it less than charming, because his expression grew grimmer by the minute.

'Why don't you leave your hair alone?' he bit off impatiently. 'You're obviously not succeeding in holding it back.'

'You are in a grim mood.'

'These past days have destroyed my sense of well-being.'

'May I ask why?' Infuriated, she allowed her hair to slide back around her face and over her shoulders.

'Since when have you been into espionage?' he asked brutally, the light shining across his high cheekbones.

'Hadn't you better explain yourself?' she exclaimed, though his question had shocked her utterly.

'Don't play games with me, Liane,' he warned, looking as remote as a total stranger. 'Convince me you haven't been passing information to Mossleigh.'

'What's going on?' Liane felt faint.

'Looking stricken won't help you!' Julian spoke with a razor-sharp accent. 'You were the only person I spoke to about my interests in Altmanns.'

Liane paused, taken completely by surprise. She could hear her breathing change. It was fearful. 'I've spoken to no one about your business interests,' she said. 'Even Barry and I don't discuss Wilde Holdings. You must know I would never interfere in any way.' She sat down quickly.

'So how would he know?'

She shook her head. 'If we're talking spies, he has them everywhere. As have you.'

'Except on this particular occasion I only spoke to you. In my absence he came here and, soon after, he started moves to foil my acquisition.'

'It has nothing to do with me!' Liane declared starkly. 'Surely you believe me?'

He made no move to check his fiery temper. He came to her and jerked her to her feet, forcing up her head so that he could stare into her eyes. 'You'd better pray I do!'

'And if you don't, what can I expect?' She gave a little broken laugh. 'Will you strangle me?'

'Not before I take you so brutally it will leave you whimpering.'

She gasped. 'I didn't do it, Julian.'

He pressed his fingers tighter around her chin. 'I've never heard you speak a lie.'

'But you don't believe me now.'

They were staring intensely into each other's eyes. 'Why did he come here?'

She swallowed against his painful grip. 'He was supposed to be in the area looking at Paradise Valley.'

'And you accepted that?'

'No, I didn't. Julian, you're hurting me.'

'Go on.'

'He came because he said he couldn't stay away.'

Julian's hand didn't move. 'And?'

'He wants to marry me. I told you that.'

'The fool! So you felt sorry for him and let it slip about Altmanns?'

'*Never*. I never let anything slip. Are you happy you're bruising my face?'

He pointedly ignored her but his grip lessened. 'What did you tell him?'

She moistened her dry lips with the tip of her tongue. 'I told him I couldn't possibly marry him.'

'And?' His sapphire eyes were raying right through her.

'And he sacked me,' she flashed. 'Are you happy about that?'

'So where did he hear it?'

'God knows!' she said huskily, and hoping for some respite slumped her chin against his hand.

'I could kill you,' he said violently and grasped her to him so powerfully her knees buckled. 'So Barry worships you, does he? He's going to dread the day he crossed me!'

'Don't be crazy!'

Though she struggled he held her. 'You look such an angel!' He twisted her long hair round and round his hand. 'No ordinary man would have a chance!'

'You know nothing about it,' she cried fervently. 'Barry is one of the most honourable men I have ever met.'

'And he's liable to get hurt if he so much as looks at my wife.'

'You should go to a psychiatrist for help. How many times do I have to remind you I'm *not* your wife.'

He wasn't in the mood to make the distinction. 'Look at me.'

'Don't I have to, you arrogant swine.'

'Is Barry in love with you?'

'That's Barry's business!' His eyes flickered dangerously. 'No, he isn't. He's drawn to me, that's all. I certainly like him. I suppose we have to thank Barbra for making trouble.'

'Barbra did mention you took great delight in each other's company'

Liane's whole body shook. 'Why did I never realise she's such a *dreadful* woman? Barry could only be a good friend to me as he is to you. I promise you, for his sake, I can find no good reason why I should have to explain myself to you; he's utterly loyal. You would insult him to even mention Barbra's duplicity.'

He laughed. 'I find your defence of him very moving.'

'It's the truth,' she said very quietly, her expression one of ineffable sadness.

'Is it? Liane!' He leaned forward and before she could move took her mouth.

Her body blazed. As his hard passion began to grow she resisted, so in the end she was a prisoner in his arms while he released his anger by crushing her mouth beneath his. She wanted to cry out, her reaction equally intense, shaking in desperation as his hand moved in possession to her breast.

'No, Julian!' Her eyes were huge with intensity and a barely concealed arousal.

'Do you think you can control *me* as you do everyone else?'

'No, Julian.' Despite herself she could feel her body respond to his cruel caress. 'Don't do this to me!'

'How can I not?' He laughed harshly. 'For reasons even I cannot understand, I can't get you out of my blood. I've been in a ferment for days thinking you may have sought to bring me down, and still I want you. I have just to look at you and you steal all my resolve away. No one, apart from you, Liane, knew about that particular venture.'

'I'm *innocent*,' she said.

'Are you?'

'What is happening to you?' she cried wildly. 'Must I pray for your sanity? Barry is devoted to you. God knows why, you're so pitiless. We're not married any more. We're *not*!'

'Then I'll make it easier for you. We'll remarry as soon as I can get a licence.' He held her arms to her side, his dark face implacable. 'I should tell you Mossleigh's curious involvement in my affairs didn't work out. I'm now well on the way to securing a thirty-percent interest in a rapidly expanding industrial group.'

'My congratulations!' She whipped her head back. 'Your secrets are safe with me for a lifetime. But I don't think you will ever win me back.'

He looked down at her, his brilliant eyes hooded. 'Don't you ever get the feeling we're chained together?'

'You alarm me, if that's what you mean. You never used to be so brutal. You never held me against my will.'

'Perhaps I will never be tender with you again,' he said wearily. 'But one thing is certain. Our long separation is over. You tried to be free of me and you didn't succeed. All this time I did not imagine you would. We're victims, you and I. Neither of us can find any peace without the other. There's nowhere you can run. No woman I can turn to for any relief. It's you I want, if I have to hound you all your life.'

'I'm going,' Liane cried emotionally. 'Please let me out of this room.'

'If I do, you should be cautious in all things. I'll accept your friendship with Barry is innocent, not that I won't be asking him a few questions, but I haven't finished my investigations into the Mossleigh affair. Someone woke him up to my plans. If you didn't do it deliberately, he must have read something into a careless remark.'

'*No* remark!' Liane tipped up her chin. 'I have the wit not to mention anything about these matters. You'll have to look to someone else other than me as your enemy. Though I dread you, you've become so hard, I wouldn't hurt you. I loved you once. You're Jonathon's father. I would as soon hurt him. You'll discover your informer elsewhere. By the way, I don't wish Barbra to remain in the house. We no longer have anything in common.'

'You wouldn't want Barbra to influence Jonathon's life?' he asked with bitter humour.

'I'll be around to watch over Jonathon.'

'That you will!'

At the ruthlessness of his expression Liane touched a hand to the beating pulse in her throat. 'Unlock the door, Julian. I don't feel I can be in the same room as you for a minute longer.'

Dinner was a most uncomfortable meal, with only Jonathon enjoying it. Even Barbra didn't risk one of her adroitly timed insinuating remarks. Barry was quite calm but quiet, and Liane for the most part kept her eyes on the table. Matters had reached a point where it was no longer safe to meet Julian's eyes. Afterwards Jonathon spent a private hour with his father who took him off to bed before sleep overcame him in a library armchair. Liane was called to say good night and at that point she fled. Julian and Barry met for a discussion that required closed doors. It was time to tackle Barbra and ask her to move on.

Barbra was discovered enjoying a brandy on the flower-filled lower deck.

'Ah, there you are, darling,' she hailed Liane's slender figure, standing beneath the archway. 'It's a bad night tonight, is it not?'

'I think you might have to take the credit for that.' Liane moved out to join her, but instead of sitting, leaned against the balustrade. 'You have a way of alienating people.'

'Isn't that a bit extreme?' Barbra looked up with dark, glittering eyes.

'I never realised you were so dangerous, Barbra.'

'Is this what I get for giving good advice?' Barbra looked deeply perplexed and hurt.

'I've always thought your concern for me was genuine.'

'My dear, you were right!'

'No, Barbra. Your motives were and remain deeply rooted in self-interest. Your friendly behaviour, the advice and understanding only made it easier for you to stir up more conflict. Think what you've done tonight.'

'Please tell me,' Barbra invited ironically, waving her balloon glass.

'You tried to get Julian to believe Barry and I have been romantically involved.'

'And that's wrong?' Barbra became roused to anger. 'How would you put it, dear?'

'You do it by *distortion*.'

Barbra's good-looking face looked set and stern. 'I simply don't know what you're talking about, Liane. Central to all this is Julian's bad effect on you. It should be clear to you by now the two of you are incompatible. I'm aware of your ambivalent attitude. You can't decide if you love him or hate him or both, but don't whatever you do, see things through his eyes. I said very little. Maybe a little joke, that's all. Certainly nothing terribly misleading. Julian himself reworked it all. He appears so tough and sane, but underneath it all I think he's a neurotic individual. Look at his treatment of you! On the one hand he won't let you get away; on the other he rejects you and your love. Men put a great deal of emphasis on possession. Julian is a very bad loser. He thinks it hardly possible you could turn away from him to somebody else. You're divorced, yet he seeks to restrict your life terribly. Don't deny it.'

'I've already noted you're clever, Barbra. We've had many of these discussions, primarily to convince me I should remarry as soon as possible to escape Julian's control.'

'Then why the delay?' Barbra challenged her. 'What are you achieving? It's hardly possible you should treat me as your enemy. I have no reason to feel guilty about anything. Maybe I was a bit naughty implying you and Barry were getting on extremely well, but why shouldn't I help you get rid of Julian once and for all? Generally that's what friends are for. You're not the only one to notice the severity of his reaction.'

'Did it never occur to you that if his anger was taken to extremes he could sack Barry on the spot?'

'For God's sake, dear,' Barbra protested wryly. 'That young man could find himself another job tomorrow. Also, if he ceased to be Julian's employee, he could assume a closer relationship with you. I'm sure that's his dream.'

'And what about your dreams?' Liane hit back. 'You're so concerned with helping other people, what is it you want for yourself?'

Barbra appeared to find that amusing. 'I live. I die. Why discuss it on a beautiful night like this?'

'Except you seem to be preoccupied with Julian. Is he your fantasy?'

Barbra laughed; an odd laugh on the edge of hysteria. 'How I loathe that man.'

'Why, Barbra? What did he do to you?' Liane spoke very quietly.

For long moments Barbra stared down into the dark amber depths of her glass. 'It all started when we were girls,' she began in an altered voice, softer, younger.

'Yes?'

'You simply can't imagine how attractive I was fifteen or sixteen years ago.'

'Oh, I can!'

'Outwardly Caroline and I were almost like twins, except Caroline was the quiet one, the passive one. At the same time, she was determined to win the handsome prince.'

'Julian?'

Barbra smiled. 'He was the handsomest, the strongest, the most brilliant prince of all! It didn't matter a damn his family had lost all their money though I recall Father was concerned about it.'

'But you both fell in love with him?'

'Along with every eligible female at that time. Julian wasn't the villain he is now. He was a hero! So tall and handsome and those marvellous eyes! I used to fantasise I was drowning in them. Bluer than the ocean, bluer than the sky. First he pretended he wanted me. I'm not being vain when I say I had a great deal more to offer than Caroline. She was the shadow to my substance. She certainly didn't have a brain. But then, when he had brought me to full life, Julian openly denied me. He dissociated himself from me entirely. He turned to Caroline. I, who could have had any other man I wanted, was cast aside. I was a stronger version of Caroline yet he chose her. Can you imagine how that made me feel?'

'Very, very angry.'

'Cast aside.' Barbra nodded several times, her expression bitter and withdrawn.

'Why did he do it?'

Barbra shrugged. 'A young man often thinks he needs a passive, clinging woman, but when he is truly mature he realises such a woman was not what he wanted at all. That's what happened to Julian, but it was far, far too late. When he turned to me I had my revenge. I scorned his every advance. As he humiliated me, I humiliated him.'

Liane couldn't easily assimilate all the information she was being fed. 'How is it Julian has never spoken of your attachment?' she demanded.

'Are you serious?' Barbra appeared to come out of her reverie. 'Why ever would he speak of it to you?'

'I suppose not.'

'Haven't you told me many times that Julian refused to speak of his first marriage?'

'I always thought that was because what happened to his wife was too painful. For a man to lose his wife in childbirth would be a crushing grief. I understood he was trying to cope with it as best he could.'

'And affirmed his grief by marrying you two years after,' Barbra declared with a terrible anger.

Liane stared at her, perturbed. 'Don't we human beings strive for a normal life? Terrible as death is, the emphasis is on life. Passion doesn't go away. Desire. Life goes on. People remarry. They always have and they always will. It doesn't mean that they don't carry their memories in their hearts.'

Barbra gave a bitter laugh. 'You and your grand-mother, what pure points of view! The fact of the matter is, Julian was consumed by guilt.'

'Because his wife died?'

'Because he *didn't love her*. It wasn't long after the honeymoon that he didn't even pretend to. For once Julian didn't see the writing on the wall. Caroline simply wasn't woman enough for him. She couldn't match him in any way. She had no passion, aggression, what you will! She was just beautiful and young. Like you. He has treated you both in the same way.'

Liane threw her an unfathomable glance. 'Yet if it is true he cared for you, why did he not marry you after a suitable time?'

'My dear girl, I have a conscience!' Barbra's thin frame was quivering with outrage. 'I could not possibly marry my own sister's husband. I had to renounce him.'

'He asked you?'

'He *begged* me, but our relationship was too close. It would have destroyed us in the end. As it was, he de-stroyed any vestige of respect I had for him. I can under-stand he wanted me, but he should never, never, have put it into words. Caroline was between us, you see.'

'And when did this take place?' Liane asked, very gravely.

'If you don't mind, my dear, I prefer not to discuss it. I'm a well-off, independent woman. I can fulfil all my needs. You are the one who cannot say "no" to Julian. I expect he has already had you in his bed? You were alone that first night.'

Liane showed her swift withdrawal. 'Whatever happens between Julian and me is private, Barbra.'

'So, you don't deny it?' On Barbra's handsome face was an expression of pure jealousy.

'What you have to do is put Julian out of your mind. You say you loathe him to everyone, yet your actions correspond to those of a woman possessed. I'm beginning to wonder how Julian found the time for all these affairs he was supposed to have. On different occasions you've mentioned a number of women, yet now you tell me all the days of his first marriage he really hungered for you. It simply doesn't add up. Barry is close to him all the time, and Barry says a lot of his playboy image is media-created. The so-called attractions simply never develop. Maybe the Press think he has no right to a private life. A close examination of the situation reveals he simply doesn't have the time.'

'Believe what you want to believe, Liane,' Barbra said in a cold, contemptuous voice. 'A child like you could never begin to understand a man like Julian.'

'Perhaps.' Liane felt a sudden, terrible desolation. Her conversation with Barbra had not marked an end to her fears, only presented more. 'Wouldn't it be better, Barbra, if you went home tomorrow?' she suggested.

'What an ungrateful girl you are!'

'I'm thinking of you, Barbra,' Liane said. 'Your intense feeling for Julian, good or bad, is making you unhappy. I'll probably make you angry, but you really do drink too much. It could develop into a problem.'

'Alas, it could!' Barbra countered very, very drily. 'A girl has to have something to relax her body.'

'You'd be better off trying a swim. Anyway, I'm not going to moralise. My intention was to ask you to leave. You may not be entirely conscious of it but you are setting destructive processes in place. I believe you worked to get Sir Eric Mossleigh up here. I also observed you two talking. I'm certain it wasn't about me.'

'And what else could it be?' Barbra asked sharply, her skin in the yellow light turning sallow.

'I'm not certain,' Liane admitted. 'Sir Eric gets an unique expression on his face when he's talking business. A kind of heightened aggression and alertness. I have witnessed it time after time. In fact, I used to think of it as his "hunter's mask".'

'Which is all very colourful but what has it to do with me?' Barbra was so angry she all but gnashed her teeth. 'I barely know the man. How could I possibly talk business with him?'

'I expect we'll find out you did.'

'My God!' Barbra was shocked out of breath. 'I can't *believe* the change in you, Liane. I thought you were different, special, now you're reacting like a viper. Next you'll be telling me I tried to foil Julian's plans.'

'Why Julian?' Liane answered swiftly, and walked towards her. 'You could have been talking about your own family's concerns for that matter.'

'This is extremely unpleasant, Liane,' Barbra announced and rose a little unsteadily to her feet. 'You're not content to ask me to leave, you wish to insult me with your vile accusations.'

'All I asked, precisely, was what you and Sir Eric were talking about so very very intently, like a pair of conspirators.'

'We were talking about you,' Barbra declared in a very flat tone. 'I never knew you could be so perfectly obnoxious.'

'When I call attention to your actions? I never found the heart to speak about all Jonathon's presents before, but you gave them to him as your own gifts.'

Barbra threw her a look of bitter outrage. 'What would you have had me do with them? Throw expensive presents away?'

'You could have told him the truth.'

'Julian wouldn't have allowed it.' Barbra studied her haughtily.

'Julian, of course, knew nothing about it.'

'Julian is a most unpleasant man.'

'Then I know you won't care to stay here any longer.'

'You fool!' Barbra shot her a glance of monstrous triumph. 'He'll betray you again.'

'Not me,' Liane answered very soberly. 'I'm changing my life.'

Both Barry and Barbra left in the morning. Barbra swept out in a fine rage without a parting word to anyone. Barry's departure brought forth the sheen of tears.

'Please tell me what Julian said to you,' Liane begged him, distressed.

'Hey, now, don't get upset,' Barry exclaimed in a comforting voice. 'I told you, Julian is absolutely straight. He shoots right from the shoulder. I haven't fallen from grace, if that's what's troubling your tender heart. Julian simply thinks it better if I go back to town.'

'But there will be no one I would want to take your place.' Liane looked deeply shaken.

'The boss will find one,' Barry drawled. 'Everything is all right, Liane. I promise you. Barbra's interference hasn't ended my career. Julian may have been briefly angry, but he has a built-in capacity for recognising the truth. Barbra played her hand and she didn't win. Believe me, you'll be much better off without her. She'll be better off without you in lots of ways. What that lady has to do is let go of the past. She's perpetuating her old griefs and resentments.'

'She told me Julian loved her,' Liane confided, secure in his loyalty. 'That he loved her even when he was married to her sister.'

'No kidding!' Barry took out a little notebook, flipped a few pages and wrote in it. 'I'd say the lady was nuts.'

'She sounded utterly sane and reasonable.'

'They usually do.'

'I know you're very shrewd and observant, Barry, but you weren't around at the time.'

'I'm around now.'

'And you don't think it true?'

'Hell, no!' Barry stared down into her lovely face. 'She's a fair terror at imparting damaging information. I'm going to do a little investigating of this lady. I should tell you it's at the instigation of my boss. Julian doesn't trust her.'

'She has always been there in the background. I don't think I told you I surprised her and Sir Eric in deep conversation. When I asked her later what they were talking about she said me, but I know in my bones that wasn't true. Certainly not at that time. I'm convinced they were talking business.'

'She did take a call from him,' Barry mused without surprise. 'A call that conveniently slipped her mind.'

'She really doesn't know him more than superficially.' Liane confirmed.

'Perhaps she found out something of value.'

'Not from me.'

'No hint, or an inadvertent word?'

'Absolutely not. I would swear on a stack of bibles. There's one in the study.'

'Sure you didn't forget to rip off a little note?' Barry asked.

'How do you mean?'

Barry frowned. 'The desk pad?'

'Well...I haven't used it.'

'I'll be damned!' He thrust his hand through his hair. 'How many times have you seen Julian sit on the edge of a desk talking? Invariably he's jotting things down as he goes. Names, phone numbers, dates.'

'I think he'd be very careful with confidential information,' Liane considered.

'He'd trust you.'

'That's sweet of you, Barry, but he doesn't.'

'Yes, he does,' Barry murmured off-handedly, staring over her head. 'What I'm suggesting is this: Julian does consider Barbra is in the house, so he tears off the top sheet and destroys it. What he omits to do is check the indentations on the next sheet. We all know Julian's firm, very self-assured script.'

'So you think someone incredibly nosy would try to decipher what he had written?'

'Why not?'

'You're writing this scenario,' Liane told him wryly.

'Miss Edwards is a very troubled woman. She's also very knowledgeable. Her father and brothers serve on any number of big public company boards. She's hooked on Julian and he doesn't want her. As a matter of fact I'd bet my entire life's savings he never so much as looked at her. This is really her kind of thing. She hates you, but she handles you very cleverly. The information on the desk pad, if handed on to someone like Mossleigh, could damage Julian and point to you. It's an opportunity too good to pass up, and it would speed things up considerably. Julian would accuse *you* and you would rush into Mossleigh's arms.'

'It couldn't happen.'

'Maybe not. Maybe not, but Barbra believed it might. Mossleigh. Me. Someone else. Who cares? So far as she's concerned, you're the only one who stands between her and Julian. Boy, was she ever a revelation! Some women just never give up. It must have been grim for her a few years ago when Julian fell in love with you. Did she make no attempt at all to break it up?'

'Lesley Bannigan did that,' Liane pointed out soberly.

'Sure the dragon lady didn't put her up to it?'

'They really weren't friends.'

Barry brooded a while. 'There's money. You'd be surprised how many people can be made to do anything for money.'

'I'm sure money wasn't a factor,' Liane said faintly. 'I've never considered that for a moment.'

'But then you're not the detective.'

'No. I'm very sorry you're leaving, Barry.' Liane began to walk with him slowly, out towards the terrace where Julian and Jonathon were waiting beside Barry's car. 'You've been a good friend to me. To Julian and his son. I'm very grateful.'

Barry's expression was a little constrained. 'Don't worry, Liane. Everything is fine. I told Julian the truth and, like a sensible man, he acted. Believe me, I'm still on the payroll. Moreover, I have a job to do.'

'If I heard you were being disadvantaged in any way...'

'Absolutely not!' he assured her. 'Please don't take Barbra's sins out on Julian. He's a fair man, Liane. I'll admit he's tough. But fair.'

'The trouble Barbra has started!'

'I enjoyed every minute.' Barry looked briefly into her beautiful eyes. 'Be happy, Liane.'

'You too. I am going to see you again?'

'Of course you are.'

'Then why is Julian sending you away?'

'Because he's smart.'

Their farewells were brisk. Jonathon, like Liane, was obviously upset to see Barry go but Julian had placated him by saying they would go sailing that afternoon.

'You're coming, aren't you, Lee?' Barry's car had sped off, now Jonathon was tugging on her hand.

'Not today, darling. You men go off.'

'But we'll miss you,' Jonathon told her, suddenly kissing her fingertips. 'Are you sad about Barry?'

'Yes, I am.'

'Dad had some things for him to do.'

'Ridiculous for you, Liane, to pine,' Julian said smoothly. 'Won't you please join us?'

'No, Julian. I won't, and I'll tell you something else.'

'Of course.' He took hold of her arm, a downright act of control.

'I would not like to ever hear Barry had lost his job.'

'No matter what?'

'No matter what!' Liane said through her teeth. 'Barry is my friend. He was marvellous with Jonathon.'

'That's fine. On that account I'm prepared to ignore his little daydream. Never fear, sweetest Liane, I'm not about to toss him out. Barry, to date, has been more a friend than an employee, and you don't find too many better. No, I have a little job for Barry. Let's say some detective work.'

'Did you see how Aunty glared at us?' Jonathon asked with perverse glee. 'Did she blame Barry, Dad, for us being late?'

'She didn't leave me wondering,' he answered drily.

'Wondering what?'

'Barry's intentions.'

'Barry's intentions,' Jonathon repeated, not understanding. 'Barry said Aunty doesn't have both oars in the water.'

Julian gave a brief, edgy laugh. 'I'm reminded someone else said something of that nature to me many years ago.'

'Who was it?'

Julian's eyes fairly blazed. 'As it happens, Jonathon, it was your mother.'

# CHAPTER SEVEN

FOR once Liane considered her own feelings. She remained at the beach house while Julian and Jonathon went sailing for the afternoon. She had no fears about both of them being out on the water. The weather was glorious and Julian had the sea in his blood. In an earlier time they had spent many wonderful hours aboard the *Lady Elizabeth* but today Liane's feelings were ragged and worn. What was Barbra, after all? The arch manipulator? The woman who so ruthlessly followed an impossible dream? Although Barbra had spoken so convincingly about intense feelings between her and Julian, Liane had a great deal of difficulty accepting it. Of course that passion had to with *then*. People changed rapidly, personalities were transformed. Yet from every account, Julian had been brilliantly mature even in adolescence. Adversity and personal tragedy had hastened the process. No matter what the complexity of his dealings with his sister-in-law, Liane's intuition, the intuition she depended upon, told her Julian felt no physical attraction towards Barbra. Neither did he appear to enjoy her personality. Their lives continued to cross because of a child. A child, moreover, who had not awakened any tender maternal feelings. The fact of the matter was, Barbra had no empathy at all with the very young. Despite her woman's body she was not motherly. She was, however, in a sexual ferment. Like Liane, she could not break free of Julian's influence. The only way to solve the problem for both of them was to take some immediate, definite action. Do something constructive like have a lobotomy, Liane thought in a kind of impotent rage.

Finally she came up from the beach, showered, changed and had Bruno Morona drive her into the resort. Shopping might take her mind off her feelings of anger at Barry's swift removal from his job. Common sense told her it was really for the best. Barry had been attracted to her, to be sure, but Julian had no right to act so decisively. He had cut her off from all contact with a friend. At least he had not been ruthless enough to dismiss Barry out of hand. He had expressed his profound doubts about *her*. In addition to being an industrial spy, she was playing his own game of mindless seduction.

A film she had particularly enjoyed, *Arthur*, presented her with an idea. She bought herself six identical swimsuits in different colours. Next she selected several beach hats all in the way of being rather expensive. Sandals followed. Somehow the attendant sensed she was getting even with some man and presented all Italian and French lines. It was a very simple matter to spend a lot of money. Julian would have to deal with the payments. She was using the credit card he had provided her with. Clothes for Jonathon followed. As a truly awful touch she bought Julian just one shirt, rose-imprinted cotton. The kind of thing you'd expect to see on Boy George.

With her purchases more conveniently packaged and left for safe keeping at the last shop, she had coffee and one delicious little chocolate liqueur confection at a bistro overlooking the ocean. All in all she felt a little better. She had always used the beauties of nature to restore her balance. The sea in particular never failed to bring about a healing. Nevertheless, she was still in a situation of danger. No matter how she fought it, no matter the anger, disillusionment and pain, she still loved Julian. No matter what he did, there was no crime great enough

to kill her love. It was unconditional. The pain of trying
to survive without him seemed to be more terrible than
being his easy prey. Obsession was alarming, and what
she felt for Julian was nothing less. She had almost
reached the stage when she thought it futile to keep
fighting him. He had established his control long ago.
Much could be said about pride, but Julian was possessed of a positive genius to deal with her every response. No matter how much she struggled to deny it
she had run out of pride so far as he was concerned.
Her love, which had once been her strength, was now
her weakness. The reality wouldn't go away. All she could
do was pretend. There was no perfect solution.

She was walking back along the main street when she
noticed a group of teenagers waiting for a bus going out
to the peninsula. There was no need to bother Bruno at
all. Probably the bus would drop her almost at the door.
She didn't mind a short walk, in any case. The scenery
was beautiful and the bush was embellished with myriad
wildflowers.

As it happened, the bus set her down a considerable
distance from the point.

'Why are you turning here?' she asked the driver in
mild agitation, only to be told she should have checked
she was on the right bus. Number 126 went to the bay.
Number 124 went to the point.

There was nothing left for her to do but walk. It
wouldn't have been so bad had she not been burdened
with rash purchases. She even had to stop to change her
medium-heeled sandals for a new pair of flatties. She
would be late.

'I don't care how late it is!' she breathed aloud. The
hotter and more tired she got, the more she reasoned
she didn't have to explain her actions to anyone. She
had been totally self-reliant in the two years since her
divorce. Most people thought of her as poised and con-

fident. She had arrived at the highly responsible position of private and confidential secretary to one of the biggest tycoons in the country. Only one person demanded she account for herself. That person was now heading her way. The car was enough: big, outrageously expensive, synonymous with power and social status.

Liane moved off the road as the big smoke-silver Mercedes 560 braked to a halt. Julian got out, slamming the door behind him.

'Where the devil have you been?' His glittering eyes took in every detail of her appearance: the flush in her cheeks and the way the damp, pale gold hair clung to her nape and temples.

'Don't worry about it, Julian,' she said crisply, tilting her chin.

'Look at you!'

'So I'm a little bit hot and bothered. Big deal!'

'Give me those things.' He put out his hand authoritatively. 'I don't understand why you had to buy out the shops in one day! You could have had all this delivered and you should have rung the house.'

'I can handle a bus ride and a walk.'

'The key is to catch the right bus. It must have left you off near the bird sanctuary.'

'It did.'

'You really like to make things hard on yourself, don't you?'

'Look,' Liane responded heatedly, 'what did you say your name was: Gadaffi?'

He didn't laugh. He took hold of her arm and escorted her across the street. 'Get in.'

'Can you wait until I get my legs in before you shut the door?' It was unfair but she didn't care.

'I thought you'd at least wear the right shoes with your dress. Since when did you wear daffodil yellow with purple?'

'I like it.' She looked down at her slender, golden legs. 'For God's sake, why do you have to treat me like a child?'

He waited until he turned the car before he answered. 'I've had a security man looking out for you and Jonathon all week. When we left you said you were going to spend a quiet afternoon on the beach. I understand you might have felt the need to get in a few hundred extra dresses, what you do not understand is, we were all worried. You told Bruno earlier you would ring.'

'So I did, but I saw the bus.'

'You look as if you've been walking for hours.'

'Thirty minutes, no more. Forget it, Julian. I'm quite safe. How was *your* day?'

'You'd have done a lot better to come with us. We enjoyed ourselves immensely, but Jonathon missed you.'

'I marvel at that love,' Liane sighed, revelling in the air-conditioning. 'You would think he was my own child. The child of my body.'

'You are the mother he needs.'

She turned her head to study his striking profile. 'You never speak about his own mother. About Caroline.'

'What do you want to know?' His tone dropped.

'Did you love her?'

'I married her, didn't I?' He glanced at her very searingly.

'Marriages are arranged all the time.'

'None of mine.'

'You're planning another?'

'Think about it and see if there's any way you can get out of it,' he retorted sharply. 'Yes, Liane, I cared about Caroline a great deal. She was warm and open and honest. She was everything her sister is not.'

'I understood they were very much alike.'

'Then you've got it all wrong. There was a strong family resemblance, but they were like day and night.

Caroline had a friendly, sunny nature. I see it in Jonathon. Barbra has a dark side to her. I always found her faintly sinister.'

'I thought maybe you were attracted to both sisters.'

His expression was hard and wary. 'Whoever has been feeding you information isn't a very reliable source.'

She waited for a moment. 'Caroline must have been very brave going ahead with her pregnancy.'

'In what way?'

She smoothed back her hair in a kind of desperation. 'Well, it was dangerous, wasn't it?'

'Yes, it was at the very end. She went right up to the last weeks before complications developed. I nearly drove her doctor mad trying to get it all out of him. There was nothing anyone could do, and believe me they worked frantically hard. Her blood pressure soared and they couldn't bring it down. I really don't want to talk about this, Liane.'

'I'm sorry to pain you but I must. I know how much you wanted children, but with Caroline's medical background...'

'What background? What in hell are you trying to say?' His blue eyes flared fire.

'Surely she was advised never to have children?'

'Oh, my God!' he said violently. 'It's my fault. We really should have had this out before. Caroline was a *perfectly healthy woman*. She had no particular problem. I should know. I just told you I spoke to her doctor frequently. Everything was progressing well. It was one of those increasingly rare things.'

'But surely all I've heard is Caroline was practically forced into having a child to please you. Moreover that it was extremely dangerous for her——'

He cut her off with more than a hint of fury. 'The trouble with you, Liane, is that you have chosen to believe everyone else but your husband. Caroline did want to please me by having a child, but neither of us had an inkling of the tragedy in store. Instead of playing judge and jury, why don't you go to her family? Her doctor?'

Liane defended herself quietly. 'It was her family who told me all about it. Barbra.'

'And you listened?' His handsome face was black with disgust.

'You would never tell me anything. When I married you, Julian, I was twenty-two. A *young* twenty-two. I had seen very little of life and human nature. I didn't believe the world was filled with dangerous people and liars. I was madly in love with you. I turned to you for everything, but that wasn't the way with you. You are and always will be supremely self-contained.'

'Oh, really?' His voice was dark with derision.

'You never would speak about Caroline. I believed you loved me but I was only a small part of your life. You had been married before and you had a little son. You never made me feel insecure but you didn't invite any discussion of your past life. I feared to intrude on your private grief. I realised the memory of Caroline was very important to you and I understand that. I wouldn't want you to forget her. I wouldn't want Jonathon to forget his mother. I think it's terrible how little attention he gets from his grandparents. From Barbra. She doesn't show much response to him either. Caroline must have been a one-off.'

'Certainly she was the pick of her family,' Julian agreed curtly. 'You have to remember Jonathon is all me. The best of me. I think once Caroline was gone they decided not to try with him. Then, after I married you...' He broke off.

'Perhaps they were frightened to open their hearts. They had suffered one terrible loss.'

'I didn't have the time to try with them, Liane, and for a while they were certainly wary of my golden girl.

I loved Caroline surely, but I was obsessed with you. You have no rival in that.'

They were arriving at the house and conversation lapsed. Jonathon raced out to greet them, smiling delightedly when Liane said she had brought him back something from the shops.

'Gosh, you did buy a lot of things,' he exclaimed, as Julian gathered the array of plastic bags from the back seat.

'My idea of punishing your father.'

'Really?' Jonathon's blue eyes rounded. 'What's he done now?'

'He doesn't have to do anything. I'm catching up.' She grasped him by the shoulders and drew him to her. 'Your nose is sunburnt. Didn't you use the cream I gave you?'

'I guess we forgot. I've had a shower and I've washed my hair.'

'Good boy!' She bent down and buried her head in his fragrant curls. 'Let's go up and open all the parcels. Your father has to wear the shirt I bought him tonight.'

Although the shirt reduced Jonathon to fits of giggles when he first saw it, his father's vivid masculinity easily vanquished sprays of roses. Julian sat at the head of the candle-lit dinner table, pretty potent stuff. Real men could wear roses after all, and just to show he didn't care he had tucked in a black and white patterned cravat at the throat. Another man would have looked ridiculous, but Julian exuded a natural elegance and sensuality. Liane was reminded of a woman photographer once calling him 'Really hot!' Perhaps his intoxicating appearance was half his problem. It drew women. A lot.

Rosa evidently thought this an important occasion, because she had created a festive meal and brought out a new, very beautiful dinner-set to serve it on. They started with the plentiful, succulent seafood: baby lobsters with a lemon-flavoured sauce, followed by a pasta dish for Jonathon because he loved it and a classic Italian beef dish served with a velvety red wine sauce for the adults. Apricot ice-cream followed served with fresh peaches and spooned over with another of Rosa's marvellous sauces.

'It will be difficult to leave here,' Liane said, as she picked up her spoon.

'You don't have to. Between one thing and another it slipped my mind. Nick has great difficulty getting here any more. He sold the property to me at the right price.'

'Are you serious, Dad?' Jonathon stared at him.

'Of course!'

'Smart you! I *love* this place.'

'Well, it's yours.'

Jonathon shook his head in amazement. 'You mean the furniture too?'

'Lock, stock and barrel!'

'Whatever that is.'

'It means everything.'

'Wow! Did you hear that, Lee?'

'Things do get moving around your father.' She knew she was being provocative, just as she had exploited her considerable assets dressing for dinner. A gauzy caftan shimmered against her skin, a swirling medley of blues and greens, silver and gold. She wore no bra and her nipples peaked subtly against the thin fabric. All along Julian had been watching her with a mixture of mockery and amusement so that an unbearable sexual tension was running down her sides. Why was she doing this? *Why?* Men and women hadn't come all that far from the primitive. She was provoking him and he was marking it. Just another example of their mutual weakness.

Liane sipped her wine while Julian's brilliant eyes moved from her face to her breast. No man learned to be so erotic. He was born that way.

'Does this mean Bruno and Rosa will stay on?'

'I intended to talk to you about it,' Julian countered very drily. 'I see no objection. Both of them are extremely pleasant and competent. Nick attests to their loyalty.'

'I like them too, but it has nothing to do with me.'

'You're not going away, are you, Lee?' Jonathon suddenly asked her with great intensity.

'No, she's not.' Julian answered with deceptive mildness. 'You've got a little trickle of ice-cream on your chin.'

'It's beaut! I helped Rosa make it. Lee's just as excited as I am. Aren't you, Lee?'

'I'm beginning to wonder if your father is not a sorcerer.'

'A magician, right?'

'Some people call it genius.'

'Want to leave this subject?' Julian invited. 'Why don't we have coffee on the terrace. I should tell you only one chocolate, Jonathon, and then we'll go for a walk on the beach. I understand you got into the habit.'

'Yes,' agreed Jonathon happily. 'Lee and Barry used to trail behind and I used to run ahead. They spent *hours* talking!'

Rosa came to serve them coffee, giving little encouraging smiles as she looked around. Those liquid brown glances spoke volumes. She obviously believed Liane and Julian were very close to reconciliation, and nothing, it seemed, would have pleased her more.

'You're going for a walk on the beach?' she asked.

'Yes, we are, Rosa,' Jonathon piped up sweetly.

'Such a beautiful night! Such a wonderful full moon!'

'A time for madness. Thank you, Rosa,' said Julian, at his charming best. 'If it were up to me I'd name you one of the great cooks of the world.

'Just make some more of that apricot ice-cream, that's all,' begged Jonathon.

The three adults exchanged an indulgent smile. With his sun-gilded skin, flower-blue eyes and silky curls, Jonathon was the sort of child who caught at the heart. It was a tremendous plus, for although the son of a very rich man, he was definitely not spoiled. He was a truly appealing little boy.

A huge copper moon hung in the sky; an enormous, seductive moon that lit up the beach and threw the high, yellow-daisy-strewn dunes into mysterious shadow. The ocean appeared flat, an infinitely calm, sparkling lake with only a froth of white where the ripples fell on to the shore.

'Oh, isn't this air marvellous?' Jonathon cried. 'Lee used to say it flew to her head like wine.'

'You and Barry must have had a good time.' Julian spoilt it all. 'I can't think of anything more provocative than that sheer caftan, but then I haven't seen those seductive sarongs. You never used to go in for overkill.'

Liane flushed. 'And who would have ever thought the great Julian Wilde could be jealous? Wait for me, Jonathon,' she called.

'No, you don't!' Julian caught her hand. 'We have a few things to discuss, you and I.'

'I think we've had one too many discussions.' Just to touch him was to walk into a trap.

He turned her towards him, eyes gleaming in the exotic light. 'You want the best thing for Jonathon, don't you?'

She threw up her head. 'I'll pass coming back to you. You are asking me, are you?'

'Absolutely. Jonathon is my first consideration in life.'

'That has been brought to my attention. What are you offering *me*?'

'Anything you want.'

'But you can't give me what I want, Julian.'

'I can give you what you want any time.'

'I'm not talking about matters sexual.'

'So why all the little messages?'

'What messages?' Her eyes flashed.

'The dress and the perfume, the shining, freshly washed hair and a hell of a lot more. I know you've got neat little breasts but you usually wear a bra. Suddenly it's off and I have to catch my breath when you walk into the room. Skip all the artful dodges, Liane. You reveal yourself to me every time.'

She reacted swiftly. 'That's your ego talking! Where women are concerned you think you're superman.'

'Don't retreat into nonsense,' he advised her crisply. 'We used to play little love games with each other.'

'Obviously mine were inadequate!'

'I didn't cheat on you, Liane,' he said curtly. 'I couldn't talk to you either. You were beyond reasoning.'

'You've still failed to convince me,' she laughed. 'If we played games I didn't understand the rules. Our ideas differed widely. I understand it's common between men and women. Shall we walk on? Who knows what's going on in Jonathon's mind?'

'Jonathon thinks you will never leave him again.' His arm slowed her pace.

'Giving you a marvellous opportunity to blackmail me.'

'Whatever it takes.'

'You admit it?'

'Hell, yes. Neither Jonathon nor I can do away with you. You've made yourself indispensable in our lives.'

'Despite your wanderings?'

'Keep on with the myth,' he said tautly. 'It's the only way you have of protecting yourself. The truth is, unconsciously you ran from me. You couldn't survive being really loved.'

'No way!' She threw back her head so that her hair flew. 'Don't try to put any of the blame on me. I may be many things, but one thing I'm not is a liar!'

'Coward. I think that says it.'

'Is it worth stressing again? *I hate you!*'

'I can break that down.'

'You haven't so far.' Yet desire was beating inside her like a frantic bird.

'Dad, Lee, what's the matter?' Jonathon ran back to them, clutching at Lee's hand. 'Isn't it time for our race?'

'Don't tell me good old Barry staged races?' Julian asked acidly, looking directly at his son.

'Of course he always let Lee win. She can beat *me* whatever I do.'

'And what did Barry do? Kiss her or shake her hand?'

'He threw flowers over her one time.'

'How cute!'

'Please Julian,' Liane warned him.

His smile made time and space tighten around her. 'God knows, I think I arrived just in time.'

Jonathon's innocent remarks marked the onset of a terrible tension. Julian's manner turned to one of extreme sarcasm, that had Liane up and moving away from him, the toss of her head setting her luxuriant hair in motion so that it swirled around her like a cloud of gold.

'I think it's time for bed, Jonathon.'

'Do I have to?' Jonathon looked up from his spectacular Lego construction.

'Yes, young man, you do. You've been on the go all day and there's always tomorrow.'

'Dad's staying, do you know that?' Jonathon went to his father, leaned against him, and put his arms around his neck. 'Goodnight, Dad.'

'Goodnight, son.' Always demonstrative, Julian returned the bear-hug with one of his own. 'Pleasant dreams. I'll think up things we can do tomorrow.'

'All I want,' said Jonathon, 'is for us to live together.'

That upset Liane so much the ready tears sprang to her eyes. She turned away quickly so that Jonathon had to run after her, catching her hand. 'Are you sick, Lee?' He stared up anxiously into her face.

'No, darling. Like you, I need an early night.'

When she came downstairs again, Julian was on the telephone and she began to walk around the house turning off the lights.

'I've got the board of directors solidly behind me,' she heard him say. 'He doesn't know just how far I've come in my progress to overthrow him.'

Liane shivered at the ruthlessness of his tone.

'You bet the gods have decided in my favour!' Julian's tone was terse and incisive. 'Don't you believe in justice, Senator?'

Liane shook her head very slowly and secured the sliding door. It didn't take much imagination to know who Julian was talking about. Eric Mossleigh was another of Julian's obsessions. If he had truly set out to destroy Julian's father, he would have to find some way of stopping his son. Julian had become a financial giant overnight.

When Julian walked back into the living-room, he didn't see her for a moment, but she saw him. His expression was riveting, both triumphant and full of a bitter regret.

'Julian!' She felt she had to let him know she was there.

'Liane,' he responded, his voice full of an exaggerated gallantry.

'I'll say goodnight.'

His brilliant eyes narrowed, but he held back an acid retort. 'There's absolutely no question you can throw yourself back into your thrilling career now.'

She forced herself to shrug lightly. 'I think I told you Sir Eric sacked me.'

'My dear girl, he only wanted you for his showpiece. The exquisite woman a rich man feels he is entitled to.'

Liane felt herself responding to his bitter mockery. 'Will there ever be a time you men allow a woman free will? Both of you appear to want me for your own reasons, but as I understand it, my wishes mean nothing.'

'Not this time,' he told her brutally. 'I'm not one of those men who think there's no substance behind a lovely face. I applaud your intelligence, Liane. In a way I'm intensely proud of you for getting through a very difficult two years, but you're a deeply disturbed young woman. On the basis of one ugly lie fed to you by scheming women and that old puppet-master, Mossleigh, you broke the rules. Rules are there for a purpose. Marriage can't be allowed to break down. Neither can family. You are and remain my wife. You can't run around pleasing yourself. Neither can I. In your case it's not even *safe*.'

'Because you're a dangerous man?' She came closer to him, tilting up her chin. Her expression was at once brave and scornful. 'Are you well on your way to smashing Mossleigh?' she challenged.

He looked angry, then amused. 'In the circumstances, my dear, would I tell *you*?'

Her lovely face whitened. 'I'm sorry. Julian,' she said, sombrely, 'living with you would be hell!'

He made no attempt to stop her as she ran up the stairs and locked herself in her room. She felt strangely dizzy. A clash with Julian would spell disaster. Even loving him how could she possibly commit herself to a new life? She would always pay the price of her perceived betrayal. Men were impossible. They expected their womenfolk to accept whatever activities they wished to incorporate into their lives. Even infidelity. Lesley Bannigan had told an entirely credible story. She had nothing to gain. Why did Julian deny it so strenuously? It wasn't like him. He was so arrogant that it would have been more like him to urge her to forget it.

'She meant nothing to me!' he could have said with a dismissive sweep of his hand. Why bother him with such trivialities as a casual affair?

Liane sighed deeply and prepared for bed. There was a way she could settle this once and for all. She had no idea what had happened to Lesley Bannigan, but perhaps she could get Barry to establish her whereabouts. She had an idea Julian was searching for her as well. It was possible Lesley Bannigan could be paid to say anything. Her mind was filled with images of Julian. His power over her was spellbinding, even when he was set on taking her over like another piece in his business empire.

Liane slipped her nightgown over her head, remembering Julian had bought it for her shortly before they had been estranged. Not that she got much wear out of her nightgowns in those days. She had only taken this one out of its box very recently. It was too beautiful to remain hidden away, ice-blue in colour with deep inserts of exquisite lace down the front. She peeped in on Jonathon who was sleeping peacefully, one hand tucked beneath his cheek. A little prayer of gratitude came to mind. They had talked over his bad experience, but Jonathon had pushed his fears away. A shift in environment had helped tremendously, but soon they would have to go back to the everyday world. What Jonathon needed from now on was a loving and aware mother and father.

How could Barbra have told such lies about her own sister? It had always seemed strange to her that Julian had not known of Caroline's supposed dangerous condition. Julian was the sort of man who involved himself in everything. Caroline's pregnancy would certainly have gained his full attention. She had been so shocked and disillusioned that she had literally fled him, caught up in her youth and extreme emotions. Now the most likely things were starting to occur to her when she and Julian were feeling at their most alienated. So many nuances to human behaviour!

Her feelings of depression had her tossing and turning until well after midnight, but gradually sleep claimed her. She always slept with the doors and shutters wide open, and the silvery moonlight stole further and further into the room as the moon sailed down the sky. Her dreams were intense and vivid, causing her to give little inarticulate moans in her sleep.

Afterwards she could never be quite sure if Julian was with her or not when suddenly a tall shadow swooped over the bed. She arched away with a frightened gasp, then Julian's arms were around her, lifting her out of the bed. She couldn't cry out though her heart was beating frantically in sudden panic.

His long purposeful strides had him across the room and out of the door she knew she had locked.

'Julian, what are you doing?' she whispered in agitation. *'Julian!'*

'Be quiet,' he warned her briefly, looking down at her lying in his arms. 'You didn't really think I was going to let you stay in your own little bed?'

His assumption of control was frightening. A tyranny!

'Put me down!' she gritted, needing desperately to be quiet. How could they possibly wake Jonathon? Though Jonathon, child-like, slept deeply right through the night.

'Make any more noise and I'll throw you out of the window.'

The night air was cool on her bare skin yet where their bodies touched heat spiralled to the surface.

'So this is the sort of man you are!'

'You ought to know,' he said darkly. 'You've made me what I am.'

They were back in his room, but instead of throwing her down on the bed he held her higher in his arms. 'You want me to make love to you or rape you? You have a choice.' A bitter humour sparkled from his sapphire eyes.

'When have I ever had a choice with you?'

'Why, you relish being made love to, you little hypocrite. You came to me a virgin but I've tapped a deep vein of sensuousness in you, haven't I?'

It couldn't be denied. 'You think I've come here prepared for intimate married life?' she cried incredulously.

'Who cares?' he laughed. 'It's high time we had our own child.'

'So I can't escape?'

'Don't cry out, sweetheart,' he hushed her unexpectedly. 'Let me make you warm in bed. Your silky skin is cool to my touch.'

'Julian, you're *not* my husband,' she said waveringly.

'Think so?' With the conscious gesture of a conqueror he stalked across the sumptuous Caucasian rug and threw her down on the bed. His dark handsome face was full of passion and drama.

'I'll never forgive you if you do this!' she threatened. 'Why do you want me when you could have anyone else?'

A tinge of amusement crept into his tense expression. 'I find myself wondering *that* from time to time. No, Liane, life is stark and loveless without you.'

'When there isn't a woman for miles around who can resist you?'

'So it's pretty sad you're the only one with any appeal for me!'

She intended to move away across the room, but need was the most powerful instinct. As his hand closed over her delicate shoulder she tilted back her throat instinctively and with a muffled groan he moved down on to the bed beside her, trailing his warm mouth from her upturned chin to the hollow between her breasts.

She drew up her legs in a kind of shuddering ecstasy and he started to gather her to him, wisps of fragrance from her body intoxicating his senses.

'My God, but you confuse me,' he whispered into her mouth, not kissing her but taking little hungry drafts from her open, cushiony lips. 'I think there's something pretty cruel about women. You fight me, send me away and lure me to you.'

Her breasts were swelling with desire. She lifted her arms and began to unbutton the shirt he wore so elegantly. His skin was dark bronze, lightly matted with dark whorls, and she scored her nails through it before clasping his lean torso and resting her golden head against his breast.

'I don't know what I want any more,' she admitted brokenly.

'You love me.'

'Yes, I did. Oh, so much. You'll never understand how much I loved you.'

'You mean you don't any more?' He took hold of a fistful of her hair and made her turn her face up to him.

'This is desire!' she said tightly.

'Oh, it is?' He stared down into her aroused face. 'What a miracle you worked that out. And desire isn't love?' His hands were moving lower over her body, electrically charging her flesh.

She gave a little moan as flutters of sensation began their tyranny. 'What is it you want of me, Julian?'

'What I had!' There was a faraway look in his deeply blue eyes. 'My shining golden girl, radiant in my love.'

'I'm not that same girl any more.'

He cupped her breasts slowly, taking their tender weight into his palms. No, you're *more* beautiful!'

'It's the truth, Julian.'

His thumbs caressed the highly sensitive peaks. 'Have I seen this nightgown before? This shimmering veil for your body?' As he spoke he slid it down until it pooled around her waist. 'You're afraid?'

'Love has many names.'

He bent his head and sought her mouth. 'I don't want you to be sad.' How could she be rational when he was drawing her soul through her tremulous lips? 'I'll only do what makes you happy.'

The tenderness was more heart-stopping than the savagery.

He had her lying back. He was leaning over her, staring down at her lovely face within the wide ash-gold circle of her spread hair. She thought she was dreaming it, because he was making love to her as he had that very first time, very slowly and tenderly making certain of her loving response. It was so rhapsodic she seemed not to be breathing. She allowed his hands and mouth to know every inch of her gleaming skin, her body blossoming as she turned towards him at his every ministration.

It was exactly as it had been long ago. She was enchanted by his exquisite gentleness. Where was the barbarian she had called him? Yet as the long moments passed, he proceeded to draw her out of this luscious soft eroticism, gratifying her less and exciting her more. Her little yearning movements, the gentle turn of her head spun out to frantic shudders, the dream turning into delirium.

'Julian!' She caught at his head, tugging on his hair, overstrung.

'I'm here, my dove.' He lifted his head upwards.

'Come to me, please.' She was almost desperate in her urgency.

'First I want your promise.'

Into her mind swam the notion he would never change.

He held her head firmly so that he could look into her eyes. 'Come back to me. We'll go through a marriage ceremony again.'

Her aroused body was screaming out for him. 'Yes!'

'You mean that?' He held her implacably.

'Yes.' She swallowed convulsively, crushed beneath him.

'There can be no going back?'

She tried to kick out in her turbulent need. 'What are you doing to me, you devil?'

'Loving you,' he returned furiously.

He needed no further urging. He entered her body with a tremendous male majesty so that she cried out as if in total subjugation. Then he began to move against her and the last vestige of control broke its bonds. They were moving into that familiar maelstrom where the circular movements took them down in an uproar, held them shuddering, then when the pressure became too much released them abruptly so that they began to soar away, bodies quivering in continuing tumult until the sensation turned to floating. Floating as though an unseen hand released them from the cords that tied them to earth.

'My love. My wife.'

Had Julian spoken or was that a voice in the swirling clouds?

'Come back to me, Liane.'

She didn't know it, but the small, exquisite space that was left to her was a faint.

# CHAPTER EIGHT

THEY were married very quietly ten days later. The ceremony was very private, with only a handful of close, trusted friends. A week after that, confirmation of their remarriage was released to the Press. For the first time in a very long time the heat of publicity was off Julian. It centred on Liane. All the old photographs were dredged up, the old gossip, and she was asked to grant interviews to several of the glossy magazines. All requests were declined. Despite Julian's much vaunted eligibility and man-about-town image, no one seemed at all surprised they had succeeded in getting together again. Julian Wilde had obviously remarried the woman he loved. Even the beautiful women who had crowded him quickly retired.

When Julian had to go to Hong Kong on business, Liane and Jonathon went with him. Neither was happy at the thought of leaving Jonathon behind so they made up a trio. Liane had visited the Orient before, each time with Julian, staying at the elegant Peninsula. Jonathon was much taken by the ornate columns in the gilded lobby and the luxury of their huge suite. The view from the rooms was endlessly fascinating, the bay crowded with all manner of boats. Jonathon particularly enjoyed watching the sails of the junks gliding so fraily past the great towering hulls of the ocean-going ships. Hong Kong was a marvellous experience for him. Liane told him Hong Kong meant 'fragrant harbour' and each time he laughed and rubbed his nose at all the inescapable pungent odours outside the hotel. The place was teeming with people, particularly noticeable to anyone coming from the vast open continent of Australia, but for all that they had a marvellous time sightseeing and taking advantage of the incomparable shopping.

On several evenings they were invited to the magnificent homes of Julian's business associates, where Liane, who was greatly drawn to Chinese porcelains, had a visual feast. On one occasion their distinguished Chinese host moved to present her with an exquisite porcelain bowl decorated in Famille Vert enamels simply because she had admired it. Although she declined the gift, not wishing to take anything so obviously old and valuable— it was of the Kangxi period, probably about the year 1700—the bowl was delivered to their hotel with the message that the brilliant blues and greens were surpassed by her eyes.

'Yuan is pretty good with a compliment!' Julian laughed.

Jonathon seemed vaguely hurt he hadn't received something so his father made up for it by buying the biggest paper dragon he could find.

It was a strangely carefree and happy time, a return to the halcyon days when they had first been married. The days were varied and exciting, crowded with experiences, the nights so sublimely romantic that Liane had a terrible fear this extraordinary harmony would not last.

They were home only a matter of days when Liane received a call from Sir Eric Mossleigh. She knew from the papers that the two men were locked in open struggle. It was the talk of the city.

'Mossleigh has to be stopped,' Julian told her. 'He worked in secret to destroy my father, but I'm doing it all out in the open. Don't spare a pitying thought for him, my love. His removal from the top will benefit a lot of people, I assure you. My father was his right-hand man, yet he ruthlessly set him up then ruined him. Friendship and a lifetime's loyalty meant nothing to him. The destruction of a family. I wonder you didn't fully appreciate it. He's power-mad.'

Under the circumstances, it was an unpleasant shock to have Sir Eric contact her.

'Right now your husband isn't in his right mind,' he told Liane. 'I want what is best for you. It's important to me that you don't get hurt.'

'So how would our meeting help anything?' Liane countered. 'Julian is my husband. My total loyalty is to him.'

'My dear, he is overreaching himself this time,' Sir Eric assured her. 'He has never run up against anyone like me before. You don't want to see him ruined, do you?'

'Right now, Julian is doing extraordinarily well.'

'Quite true!' Sir Eric chuckled humourlessly. 'But I have inside information that would put him right in a corner. I'd have no trouble ruining him, but for you. He has no right to have such a wife, but you lost your nerve. You couldn't hold out against him. What I am proposing is you call in and see me at the office. We'll have lunch in the boardroom. I believe I was your friend when you wanted one. I still am. Besides, there's a little business we still have to discuss. You have never collected the money due to you. Please say you'll come, Liane.'

'Sir Eric, I'm sorry. Julian would not approve.'

He laughed quietly into the telephone. 'And you do everything you're told.'

'I do not associate with my husband's enemies.'

'I remember a time when your husband was your enemy,' he retorted sharply. 'I was your friend. I think you owe me this courtesy, Liane.'

Momentarily she was confused. Some issues were never black and white. Sir Eric had been a good friend to her when she most needed it.

'All right,' she agreed quietly.

'Lovely! Allow me to send the Rolls for you. Shall we make it one o'clock Wednesday?'

Liane fully intended telling Julian, but she was loath to allow talk of Sir Eric to come between them.

Jonathon, who was starting a new school in the coming term, watched her dressing. 'I wish I could come with you.'

'Not today, darling,' Liane said soothingly. 'I have to talk to someone.'

'Who?' Jonathon demanded. 'Dad says I have to keep an eye on you.'

'Pardon me?'

Jonathon laughed. 'You know when you were dizzy?'

'Jet-lag.'

'Dad talks to me all the time. He tells me I must see you're all right and if you're not I'm to ring him.'

'Darling, boy! I'm as fit as a fiddle.' Liane stood up, surveying her slender figure in the long mirror. She was wearing a stylish lapis-blue suit. 'How's that?'

Jonathon nodded. 'You look great! Didn't you tell me someone was picking you up?'

'That's right.' Liane slipped a silver bracelet on her arm.

'So who is it?'

Liane looked at him and saw he was more than just curious. In view of his experience she decided to tell him the truth. 'Sir Eric Mossleigh has asked to see me.'

'And you're going?' Jonathon looked at her in bewilderment.

'I figured it was easier to get it over and done with. I was his secretary for two years, and there are a few matters still to be cleaned up.'

'Like what?' Jonathon was as decisive as his father. 'Don't go, Lee. Dad wouldn't like it.'

Liane stared at him. 'I don't want to go, but Sir Eric has never given me any cause to dislike him.'

'He asked you to marry him, didn't he?' Jonathon offered in disgust.

'That's supposed to be a compliment.'

'Dad didn't see it that way.'

'I know, darling, but I'm my own woman, despite the fact no one pays any attention. I don't know whether you can understand this, but I feel I owe Sir Eric this one visit. A sort of cutting of the ties.'

'I think it's a big mistake,' Jonathon announced with a maturity that surprised her. 'Dad says he's a crook.'

'That may be correct, but I never knew about it. I should be no more than two hours at the outside.'

'*Two hours!*' Jonathon mourned. 'Ten minutes is plenty.'

'You *are* your father's son.'

'I'm your son too, Lee.' Jonathon leaned against her. 'Do you mind if I call you Mum?'

'Oh, how beautiful!' Liane was so surprised and moved the tears rushed into her eyes. 'I would love you to call me Mum, darling. You know I think of you as my own precious boy.'

'Then don't go, Mum,' Jonathon said smartly.

Liane leaned to kiss him. 'I promise you I'll get my business over and leave in a hurry.'

'The man is a rotter,' Jonathon announced shortly. 'A real shocker.'

'Rotter? Shocker?' Liane stared at him.

'I heard someone say that from the top of the stairs. It isn't hard to hear, you know.'

'Particularly when you're listening. You appear to be a young man who keeps his eyes and ears open.'

'Sure thing, Mum,' Jonathon said softly. 'Dad has complete confidence in me.'

He insisted on seeing her off and stood at the door with Bateson, the major-domo. Usually he waved and smiled sweetly. Today he was obviously doubtful. Bateson, towering over his small figure, looked the same.

For the first time Liane felt like a trespasser in the Mossleigh stronghold. She was escorted to the executive offices, watched by dozens of avid eyes. Quite a few people knew she had been more to Sir Eric than a valued secretary, in fact some people who revelled in groundless gossip hinted that she might have been his mistress. The feud between Sir Eric Mossleigh and Julian Wilde was now out in the open and the financial world was lining up in camps. As a perceived pawn between them, Liane had reached celebrity status. Her blonde beauty had long accustomed her to being stared at, but this was different. She was made to feel the woman in between.

Sir Eric greeted her with a kiss on the cheek and took her hand.

'You look perfectly beautiful, my dear,' he said sincerely. 'We might as well go into the boardroom now. I've organised a light lunch. Everything I know you like.'

'This is rather an awkward situation, isn't it, Eric?' Liane said when she was seated.

'Never awkward with you, my dear. I had had such a wonderful life planned for us, then Wilde got in the way.'

'I love him, Eric.' Liane looked down at the magnificent emerald on her left hand.

'I know you do, my dear. That's your cross.'

'Please . . .'

'I know. I know. I can control myself. As a matter of fact, I'm trying to work out a way Wilde and I can stop all this mudslinging.'

Liane frowned. 'I don't know that you can call it that!'

'Nevertheless it's dragging us down. Losing his father was an enormous trauma for Wilde. He was young and he has never got over it.' Sir Eric broke off as the caterer entered the room. White wine was served, a crisp Chardonnay, the perfect accompaniment to crab with a piquant sauce, but Liane wasn't interested in food.

The entrée had no sooner been served than Sir Eric went back to the situation that was plaguing him. 'You know Wilde's very friendly with Senator Jim Grant?'

'Yes, I know Senator Grant,' Liane agreed cautiously.

'There's talk that they want Wilde to go into politics.'

'I can't discuss Julian's affairs, although it's true he has been approached. It was in all the papers.'

'How do you feel about that?' Sir Eric asked her, eyes keen and searching.

'I'll agree to anything that will benefit my country. Provided Julian wanted to change careers, that is. He has a great deal to offer.'

'I may be able to help him there.' Sir Eric nibbled on his moustache.

'Julian is his own man, entirely.' Liane pointed out.

'Of course you know he blames me for his father's crash?' Sir Eric looked up quickly from beneath beetling brows.

'I'm unhappy to tell you he does.'

He grunted. 'There are many things I could speak of but it would only make matters worse. Suffice it to say, I am blameless in the Wilde affair. Jonathon Wilde took a great risk. He put himself out on a limb through greed. It's the old story. An ounce of luck and he might have been able to pull it off. As it happened, he crossed me and ruined himself. I should warn you the same thing looks like happening to his son.'

'No, Eric,' Liane contradicted quietly. 'Julian is not going to lose this fight, and I think you know it. That's why you're so worried. I worked for you long enough to read your expressions.'

'Of course it's the sort of thing the public loves!' Sir Eric veered off angrily. 'Wilde is a traitor to the business community.'

'Many of whom seem to be lined up behind him.'

'It has certainly helped him that you two have come together. A good and beautiful wife is a great help to a man in a top position. He managed to overcome the scandal the last time but it appears there's even more that could come to light.'

Liane set down her fork, her expression determined. 'I came out of past loyalty. But if you continue in this vein, I must go.'

There was a tap at the door and Sir Eric looked up, rather eagerly Liane thought. 'Ah, Miss Edwards!' He rose to his feet.

'Barbra!' Liane turned around suddenly, feeling as though the room was spinning.

'Surprise, surprise!' Barbra, looking severely elegant in black and white, walked calmly into the room. 'I'm so sorry I'm late. I got caught up in the downtown traffic.'

'No matter!' Sir Eric returned suavely, holding out a chair.

Liane felt herself colouring with anger. 'Obviously this was prearranged.'

'It has to be done, dear. Unpleasant as it may seem. Someone has to stop this crazy war.'

'Not me.' Liane pushed back her chair and stood up.

'Think what might happen to dear Julian if you go?' Barbra's dark eyes glittered.

'Julian can look after himself.'

'Not this time!' Barbra announced with considerable satisfaction. 'I know he doesn't mind anything for himself but he would mind a great deal about you. His spotless lily. The tabloids are lapping up all they can get about the prince and princess of commerce.'

Liane got to her feet, she didn't know how. Her dizziness that came and went seemed much worse. 'I can't believe this of you, Eric,' she said.

'Sit down, my dear.' Sir Eric appeared both harassed and unhappy. 'I have to use anything, *anything*, to stop your husband.'

'You're crazy to use Barbra. You see, she's almost mad!'

'Mad!' Sir Eric gave a barking laugh.

'She has lied to me over and over again,' Liane answered, 'and to my everlasting shame I never doubted her for a moment.'

'Take a hold on yourself,' Barbra urged tauntingly.

Liane stared down at her, like an angel at the Last Judgement. 'Do you remember telling me your sister should never have had a child? That it was dangerous?'

'Quite true,' Barbra chided lightly.

'Totally untrue,' Liane returned in a hollow voice. 'I have seen her medical file.'

'So?' Barbra gave an expletive of impatience.

'You must have been enjoying yourself preparing the groundwork. Your ultimate plan was for Julian and me to divorce, but first you were going to see that my love was torn into little pieces.'

Barbra laughed again. 'It worked.'

'Now just a minute,' Sir Eric intervened, his handsome face reddening.

'No, you wait a minute,' Liane replied coolly. 'For years I admired you, now it seems you're utterly committed to protecting your empire no matter whom you destroy and whatever the outcome.'

Sir Eric, too, stood up. 'It's obvious you know nothing about power.'

'Believe me, I don't think I *want* to know. If you think the lies of a mad woman give you grounds for attacking my husband...'

'Look, darling, we're going to attack *you*,' Barbra laughed, malice flaring in her eyes.

Liane stared at her. 'Then go right out and do it. All that matters to me is Julian's love. God forgive me for ever doubting it. There was no Lesley Bannigan, was there?'

Barbra regarded her triumphantly. 'A wonderful little affair built right out of air.'

'And how did you get her to confess? She must have known it would ruin her own marriage.'

'My dear,' Barbra pointed out, very drily, 'her marriage was over. Lesley played the field, but not with your high and mighty husband. All I had to do was show her money.'

Sir Eric was startled. 'You mean *you* did all this? *You* chose as your victim an innocent young girl?'

Barbra looked at him sharply. 'The innocent are the best victims, as we both know.'

'Dear God!' Sir Eric heaved a troubled sigh. 'I had no knowledge of this, Liane. None at all. As I understood it, Wilde had become a womaniser.'

'What a joke!' Barbra looked up at them, more amused than deeply shamed. 'I tried and I failed. The only real problem was Julian. I had dear sweet little Liane out of the way. I doubt if she would have become a serious contender ever again. Except for Julian. He just couldn't free himself of her. Eradicating an obsession is not an easy thing to do. She is his symbol of everything good in life. The fool loves her.'

'But what did you hope to gain?' Sir Eric asked in puzzlement.

'Julian,' said Liane.

'Why?' Sir Eric shook his head. 'Everything she tells me would seem to indicate she hates the man.'

Liane regarded him gravely. 'Some women are bred to these perverse passions. Surely, for such a clever man, you could recognise the signs?'

'*You* didn't,' Barbra pointed out with gloating satisfaction.

'I'll admit it. I was a child compared to you. But I've learned. I didn't realise a woman could direct hatred at the man she loved. That she wouldn't hesitate to destroy his happiness. Not only his happiness but the happiness of his little son. Her nephew, in fact.'

Barbra shrugged. 'I seem to be empty of all remorse. I played for high stakes and I lost. There is suicide, who knows?'

Sir Eric turned on her explosively. 'There is a job of work. I detest women of your type. In your case money and leisure corrupt. Why don't you get out there and try and earn a living? There's far more to life than playing your vicious, feline games.'

'Well, well!' Barbra's good-looking face twitched with genuine amusement. 'Who better to ask than a man who intends to be my partner?'

Sir Eric's face froze. 'Proceeding with any of this is out of the question.'

'Thank God.' Liane looked round for a chair and slumped into it.

'How do you do it, darling?' Barbra asked with real interest. 'You're such a fool, you don't know you have *real* power.'

'Frankly,' Sir Eric said, 'I think *you're* the fool. You've wasted your life on a dream. Why don't you now forget it? There's still time. Good heavens, woman, you presumed a great deal if you thought Wilde had any interest in you.'

For the first time Barbra showed her turbulent sub-conscious. 'What would you know?'

'What you told other people were your private dreams and fantasies. It's pathetic!'

'And what do you know about jealousy or love?'

'Enough not to allow it to destroy me or the object of my love. I would have to make do with friendship and respect. For the first time in my life I know fear.' Sir Eric faltered and sat down. 'It would require some ugly tricks to stop Wilde, but I now find I can't do it. Let him get on with ruining me. I did it to his father.'

'You admit it?' Liane's lovely eyes reflected her pity and sadness.

'Things became so very, very complicated at the time. I had to move swiftly, with no time to think at all. Someone had to be the scapegoat. Jonathon Wilde was perfect. Because he trusted me. In a way my life has come full circle. I stand on the very brink of ruin. Your husband has done that to me, as I knew in my bones he would. He loved his father and it happened at the worst time of his life. His adolescence. I know he swore revenge.'

'So our plan is abandoned?' Barbra rasped.

'It is indeed,' Sir Eric replied in a profoundly calm voice. 'I was going to try to get you to stop your husband, Liane. Miss Edwards has photographs of you and some security fellow at the beach house. Knowing you, I re-alise they are quite innocent, but they mightn't appear that way in the papers. The chap, for instance, is always turning to you like a lover.'

'My God, Barbra!' Liane's eyes flickered. 'You were taking photographs?'

Barbra nodded. 'I think they're quite good.'

'Fortunately I have them and the negatives,' Sir Eric returned suavely. 'I shall destroy them Liane, in your presence. I've always been a ruthless man, but when put to the test I can do nothing to harm *you*. Your husband, yes. Men have to expect battle.'

'You twister!' Barbra leapt to her feet. 'You tricked me.'

'It looks like it.' Sir Eric's face hardened. 'What do I have to pay to get rid of you? Whatever it is, it's worth the price.'

'I'll think of something,' Barbra snapped. 'All this because you want to stay darling Liane's white knight?'

Sir Eric made a dismissive motion with his hand. 'I'm not worth it.'

Barbra's look of outrage became calculation. 'I'm comfortably off, but everyone likes money.'

'I think it's time I left,' Liane said quietly. 'Thank you, Eric, it's in us all to make amends.'

Sir Eric rose to his feet. 'There's nothing to thank me for.' He took her hand and held it and as he did so the door burst open and his secretary cried out in agitation,

'This isn't *my* fault, Sir Eric. I told them you weren't to be disturbed.'

Julian strode into the office holding Jonathon by the hand. He smiled, the uncivilised smile of a Genghis Khan. 'Are you ready to come home, Liane?' he asked.

She went straight to him and Jonathon grasped her hand. 'I rang Dad,' he told her in a loud stage whisper.

'My wife deserves my help,' Julian said acidly. 'She's the victim of an exceedingly tender heart. May I ask what *you're* doing here, Barbra?'

Barbra's usual arrogant expression held more than a hint of fear. 'And why not?' she countered lightly. 'Sir Eric has been kind enough to offer me a job. Nothing definite yet but I know there could be something suitable in public relations.'

'You must be close to starving after all the money you've handed out. That was a considerable sum you paid Lesley Bannigan.'

'The bitch insisted.' Barbra kissed a hand to him. 'I hope she's holed away where I can't get to her.'

'She's a very greedy woman.'

'Greedy people will do anything. You know that. Now, my dears, you simply must excuse me. I have to leave. How are *you*, Jonathon?' Barbra turned to smile at him.

'I'm quite well, thank you, Aunty,' Jonathon responded politely.

'You're a great kid, do you know that? Summoning your father! You have plenty of spunk.'

'Thank you again, Aunty.'

'I'd never hurt *you*, Jonathon.'

Jonathon gazed straight up at her. 'You must never hurt Mum and Dad. I'm small now, but I'll get big.'

Barbra laughed in genuine amusement. 'A chip off the old block!' She put out a hand and ruffled Jonathon's curls. 'See me out, Eric, would you? We still have one or two matters to discuss.'

They journeyed home in silence. Jonathon sat big-eyed in the back holding Liane's hand. Julian sat in front with his chauffeur.

'I guess Dad's mad,' Jonathon whispered into Liane's ear. 'I wonder what he said to Sir Eric. They were an awful long time.'

'Poor Sir Eric,' Liane said miserably. 'He reminded me of a dragon without all his fire-breathing equipment.'

Very wisely, Jonathon went straight to the games room and set up a battle between his toy soldiers. Julian followed Liane upstairs to their bedroom.

'You want to tell me what that was all about?' he asked directly, his handsome face stern.

'I will when you settle down.' Liane moved slowly because she was still dizzy, removing first her shoes then her jacket before she lay down on the bed.

His eyes flew to her in concern. 'What is it?' He went to her immediately, staring down at her with his intense blue eyes.

'My God, Julian, you can't be serious. You charged into that office like some warlord of old. I'm sure if you had had a sword you would have used it. I'm a little frayed out. I'm tired of standing around like some idiotic medieval lady watching the men fight over me. I can take care of myself!'

He sighed, his anger defeated by her apparent fragility. 'I'll have to try and remember. I was so furious when Jonathon called me.'

'And there's another one!' Liane protested. 'My own little Jonathon is all set to follow in his father's footsteps. Not one of you thinks I'm strong enough to stand on my own two feet.'

'You're lying down now, darling,' Julian pointed out. He sat down beside her, cupping her face with his beautiful hands. 'We love you. Can't you understand that? We love you and want to protect you from all harm. You can't deprive a man of his natural instincts. The male role.'

'And I wouldn't want to,' Liane murmured, relieved the harshness was dying out of his expression. 'But I fear you sometimes, Julian. You look so formidable.'

'Darling girl, I'm not a man to beat about the bush. My enemies had better know that.'

'And what about Sir Eric?' she asked him.

His sapphire eyes glinted. 'Surely you're not pleading for that old devil?'

'I've tried to despise him,' she confessed, 'but I can't. When it came down to it, he couldn't hurt me. No matter how much you've got him on the run.'

Julian nodded. 'You realise, of course, that I could finish him off now?'

'Are you ruthless enough to do it?'

'Oh, yes,' Julian assured her, looking at her hungrily. 'Let him suffer awhile.'

Her eyes filled with tears and she turned her head away from him along the lace-edged pillow. 'It's up to you, Julian.'

'No, darling, it's up to you.' He turned her face back to him, looking down at her with such loving tenderness she caught her breath. 'If you want me to let up on the old villain, I might. At the very least, he's been badly hurt.'

She could see the physical urgency in his eyes. 'Can't the bitterness end?' she asked very quietly. 'I don't want you to turn into another Sir Eric, and even he turned away from the edge.'

'Only for a woman,' Julian pointed out, looking suddenly grim. 'You're there between us. Neither of us, it seems, can bear to hurt you.'

'You can work something out, can't you?' said Liane, taking his hand and guiding it to her breast. 'You have a tremendous opportunity to be merciful. If you destroyed him, you wouldn't win anyway. You would be doing damage to yourself. Vengeance is terrible.'

'I accept that.' He caressed her. 'But up until now I just didn't care. He spoke to me about those times. He didn't try to whitewash himself. He gave it to me straight. It was he or my father, as he saw it. He couldn't throw away what he had built up.'

'But you've taken it from him all the same.'

'He acknowledges the justice.'

'Then isn't that enough?' The touch of his hand was exquisite.

'We'll see.' He bent to kiss her. 'Enough of Mossleigh,' he whispered huskily, 'what about you?' He traced a finger along a blue vein. 'You said there was something you wanted to talk to me about tonight. Something special.'

'I think it is.' They were together. Nothing else mattered.

'Fire away, Mrs Wilde. I should be returning to the office but I don't think I will.' He drew her to him with a groan. 'Will you ever know how much I love you, my special girl? I wish to God we could discard these clothes.'

'As I see it,' Liane began, 'Jonathon needs a little sister.'

He drew back immediately. 'You're pregnant?'

'I'm so perfectly, *perfectly*, happy.'

'My darling!' He gathered her to him in an ecstasy of elation. 'I just don't believe it. It's what...?'

'I can't answer exactly, but I would say the very first time we came back together.'

Love and pride were intense in his eyes. He took her hand and kissed each one of her fingers in turn. 'This is wonderful news.'

'Yes, it is.' She smiled at him with a little onrush of tears.

'I was going to make love to you,' he told her a little unsteadily. 'I suppose there's no chance?'

'Not this afternoon,' she murmured regretfully, but drew his dark head down to her. 'But there's always to-night. Can you come home early?'

'I'll run.' He lowered his mouth to hers, his blue eyes aflame.

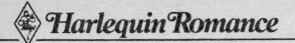
# Harlequin Romance

## Coming Next Month

**#3001 UNCONDITIONAL LOVE Claudia Jameson**
Coralie's new life in Salisbury is disturbed when Jake Samuels and
his son arrive and Jake offers her a decorating commission. Coralie
knows she can handle the arrogant Jake, but she's convinced
something's wrong in the Samuels household.

**#3002 SEND IN THE CLOWN Patricia Knoll**
Kathryn, as her alter ego Katydid the Clown, had been adored by
thousands. But as Reid Darwin's temporary personal assistant life is
no circus. What did she have to do to win even a word of praise
from her toughest critic?

**#3003 BITTERSWEET PURSUIT Margaret Mayo**
Charley isn't looking for romance—she just wants to find
her father. Yet thrown into constant contact with explorer
Braden Quest, who clearly opposes her presence on the jungle
expedition in Peru, Charley is aware of the intense feelings sparking
between them....

**#3004 PARADISE FOR TWO Betty Neels**
Prudence doesn't regret giving up her own plans to accompany
her godmother to Holland. She finds her surroundings and her
hostess charming. However, she can't understand why the arrogant
Dr. Haso ter Brons Huizinga dislikes her—and tells herself she
doesn't care!

**#3005 CROCODILE CREEK Valerie Parv**
Keri knows returning to the Champion cattle station can mean
trouble—yet her job as a ranger for Crocodile Task Force requires it.
Meeting Ben Champion again is a risk she must take—but it proves
more than she'd bargained for!

**#3006 STILL TEMPTATION Angela Wells**
Verona is happy to accompany her young friend Katrina home to
Crete, but her excitement is dampened by Katrina's domineering
brother, Andreas, who expected a middle-aged chaperone, not an
attractive young woman. Suddenly Verona's anticipated holiday
turns into a battle of wills....

**Available in September wherever paperback books are sold,
or through Harlequin Reader Service:**

In the U.S.
901 Fuhrmann Blvd.
P.O. Box 1397
Buffalo, N.Y.  14240-1397

In Canada
P.O. Box 603
Fort Erie, Ontario
L2A 5X3

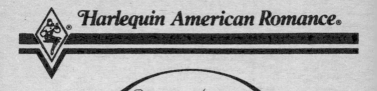

# LOST

**MOON FLOWER**

TO BE FOUND...
lots of romance & adventure
in Harlequin's
3000th Romance

## THE LOST MOON FLOWER
### Bethany Campbell

Available wherever Harlequin Books
are sold this August.